poor among riches,
wretched in the midst of splendor . . .

Never has the impulsive generosity,
the compulsive selfishness of a beloved
public figure been so strikingly
revealed as in this poignant story of
a woman with the world at her feet,
and of her heartbreaking,
heartwarming meeting with the
child they had taken away
from her long ago . . .
Never has the paradox of the
Performer been caught so
stunningly as in this novel by the
master storyteller, John D.
MacDonald, based on the motion
picture starring Judy Garland.

i could go on singing

by john d. mac donald

an original gold medal book

gold medal books
fawcett publications, inc., greenwich, conn.
member of american book publishers council, inc.

i could
go on
singing

one

THROUGH THE WINDOW at his elbow he saw the last misty halo, a small pink-white radiance of metropolitan millions, inconsequential as swamp fire, sliding away and behind as the jet tilted, climbing to authorized altitude for the eastward flight across the Atlantic, rushing toward the sun at half the speed of light, a sun which by now, he estimated, was dawning over Moscow and would meet him on this March morning in Paris.

With a wryness of self-knowledge, he knew this was one of his small devices, one of his attempts to bring order into a world which became increasingly erratic, insensible and forlorn. And this mission, he knew, would require of him every balancing and restoring device he could muster, although his sure instinct for his own breaking point was telling him that maybe it would not be enough. Not this time. Not when your own past is such a merciless part of the equation.

His name was Jason Brown, and he was in his thirties, a limber and indolent-looking man, concealing ulcerous tensions behind a lazy-eyed equanimity, a knuckle-jointed man with a used, pebbled, furrowed face, each fresh suit irreparably wrinkled the moment he put it on, shock of brown hair springing to disorder as soon as the comb was put down, pipe spewing ashes.

The stewardess brought his drink, and he sipped it and looked toward the night and saw his reflection in the glass and marveled that the face, as familiar as old shoes and jackets, should look the same as always.

He lifted his glass and said to himself, "Down with this revolting, idiotic mess. Down with Jason Brown. Down with traps, subterfuge, conspiracy, and especially down with Sid Wegler."

The trouble with people like Wegler, he reflected, they always detected your vulnerabilities, then used them against you. But that was very probably one of the essential skills

7

of the head of a large movie studio, the ability to get the maximum use out of the Jason Browns of this world.

And the basic vulnerability was money, as always. And his own incomparable credulity. He had walked right up to stand on the trap door, and Wegler had pulled the string. Smiling.

If, three weeks ago, anyone had tried to tell Jason Brown that he was going to become involved again in any way with Jenny Bowman, he would have said firmly that it could not possibly happen. Yet here he was, hurtling toward Sunday morning, toward the ancient dignified grubbiness of London, toward the London Palladium where Jenny was doing a charity concert this coming evening prior to her London opening.

In retrospect he knew he should have been wary when Wegler had phoned him directly in Santa Barbara, where he was living and working in his sister's house, and said affably, "Jase, you're the one can work the bugs out of this cruddy script we got so much money in already, I got to salvage it or look very bad, that is if you can pull loose from whatever you're working on. Just checking to make sure before I send one of my smart boys to dicker with your smart agent, fella."

Creative man is forever gullible. He feigned reluctance. Sandy, the agent, worked the studio for a sixteen-week contract at enough a week to make Jason Brown feel as if he had suddenly walked out of a damp cave into refreshing sunlight. When, on his first day, Wegler made him wait only twenty minutes, then greeted him with effusive cordiality in his big office and gave him a copy of a Headly Jamison script, an original, Jason should have felt the first tickle of wariness. Not that his creative record was entirely meager. There was one fair play, and one reasonably solid novel, and the listed credits in radio, television and moving pictures. But there were also the plays that never worked, the novels that died quietly, and the numerous credits that emitted a small sharp odor of hack. When you chop and change and rework the original efforts of others, that flavor is almost inescapable.

There had been the years when the money came in very nicely, and he had spent too much of it. And, of late, he had committed a few tactical errors. He had become too confident of the book he was working on, and had side-stepped a few too many television assignments in order to work on it, and then had seen the book slowly going sour, had gotten too anxious about it, and had lost his sense of certainty about what was needed to retrieve it. And four-year-old Bonny was his hostage to fortune.

And so Wegler's offer had been such a timely windfall, he had not stopped to think that in the normal course of events one does not hire a Jason Brown to salvage a Jamison script. They gave him a pleasant office, efficient equipment, ample supplies and access to a secretary.

And he went to work on the script, looking for the flaws he expected to find. He read it over and over. He made notes. He marked passages. He told himself this scene could be tightened, and that motivation could be strengthened, and these stretches of dialogue could be smoothed out. But after three days of it, he knew he was kidding himself. As far as he could see, it was the best thing Jamison had ever done. It had originality and power. It had scope and persuasion and great dramatic impact. He knew he was enough of a craftsman to be able to tinker with it in minor ways and effect a few minor improvements. But if the studio heads thought it needed a major salvage job, they were out of their minds.

The Jamison script was called *The Longest Dawn*. As is, solidly cast, produced and directed, it could bring down a golden rain of Oscars, and he had too much respect for decent work to chop into it, knowing he would only diminish it. And so, on his fourth working day he tried to make an appointment with Sid Wegler. He tried for a week without success, and finally composed a long memorandum to Sid, stating his views. He cut the memo down to three paragraphs and sent it along, appending the few changes he had made in the script. He visited Sandy's office and told him what he had done and showed Sandy a copy of the memo. As he had expected, Sandy called him a damned fool.

There was no response from Sid Wegler. The day before yesterday Wegler had called him in. Sid was a lean, bald, bland man. He could look thirty-five or sixty-five, depending on his mood. He used long silences as a weapon of discomfiture.

"Jase, sit down and let's thrash this thing out. I was heartened by your memo. Truly heartened. It is the kind of integrity I would expect from you."

"Who had the idea anything was wrong with the script?"

"My boy, in this business if we could be sure of anything, we would all be stinking rich. Little doubts creep in. Is there an audience for a mature, adult, significant story like *The Longest Dawn*? Should it be hypoed a little? You are on contract to work on this script, Jase, and you are going to live with it."

"But there's nothing I can do to it, Sid."

"Have you examined it from all angles? I say no. I say you have not. Because there is a factor, a very important factor, which must be fitted into this equation, Jason. And that is the factor of the star. Am I right?"

"Any actress worth beans would give up eternal salvation to get her teeth into this."

"But some ways of doing a scene play right for one and should be changed for another. There is a fitness about these things. And though we have provisional script approval, I want you to work this whole thing out very very carefully with the star. Are you willing?"

"Of course, Sid, but isn't that the director's business?"

"In this case there are a few little problems. Emotional, psychological, you name it. I keep frictions down. Friction costs money. In this case, it seems to me best that you handle it, go over it with her, prepare recommendations which will guide the director."

"Who is the lucky girl?"

There had been an odd flicker in Wegler's eyes, immediately explained when he said, "Jenny Bowman."

Jason Brown had found himself standing, trembling, his voice uncertain. "Now *wait* a moment!"

"Don't jump around. This is a quiet talk between friends. A professional talk, Jason. How many years ago was it? You and Jenny were very close. Six? Seven?"

Jason sat down. "Seven years ago," he said in a dull voice.

"You wrote the screenplay, worked along on the shooting, Jenny starred. A solid little picture. Nothing exceptional. It made a dollar." Wegler's voice softened. "In this business so many tensions, erosions of ego. Take Jenny's two marriages, for example. They ended in hate and despair. But after you were close, you and she parted in friendship, warmth, perhaps gratitude. Who can say? But a good relationship, a civilized way for things to end. Even, we might say, an adult way."

"How would you know that?"

Wegler shrugged. "Somebody said she speaks well of you."

"Did you know this . . . I mean did you have this in mind when you phoned me in Santa Barbara three weeks ago?"

"How could I help it, dear boy? You were hired to work on a script starring Jenny Bowman. The association was inevitable. I was aware that she trusts you, and trusts your judgment. I remember something about your prying her loose from a financial adviser who was robbing her blind."

"You're too well-informed for this to be entirely casual, Mr. Wegler."

"What happened between you and Jenny?"

After a thoughtful pause, Jason said, "I'll tell you only because it will give you the reason why I'm not the one to go see her about this script. She was vulnerable. She was on the rebound from that first miserable marriage and that scabrous divorce, and her nerves were raw. She was sick unto death of public personalities, and she thought she saw in me a . . . a kind of strength and stability and quietness that she thought she wanted. She didn't see me as I am. She saw what she thought she needed, and so I tried to be what I thought she needed. At best, it was an impersonation. She wanted to lean on somebody, and I was perfectly willing, like a damned fool, to tell her what she should do with her life. When the picture was in the can, we went down to Acapulco for a few days. We planned to be married. We both believed it would work out. We nearly got married in Mexico, Sid. But we decided to wait until she finished some television things in New York and a short personal appearance tour. I went with her to New York, but I had to come back here when she went on tour. What happened to us was that we were both wrong about each other. She bought my imitation of strength and certainty and control. And what I didn't realize about her was that I had met her when she was as low as she ever gets. The emotional strain and the working strain had worn her down to a shadow of her normal self. But never having known her when she was up, I couldn't see it. She was trying to hide from the world and from herself, and I thought that was the normal Jenny Bowman. But she started to recover in Mexico, and she was more like her normal self in New York, and by the time she had finished the tour, she was herself again, all that fabulous incredible energy, all that outgoing warmth and joy and confidence, loving the people milling around her every minute. I soon realized that I could only be peripheral in her life, an appendage, a Mr. Jenny Bowman. She wasn't looking for my strength any more, and when she stopped looking, the imitation collapsed and she saw me as I am, a sort of uncertain guy, mildly neurotic I guess, often confused, too emotional about some things and not emotional enough about others. But I do know I helped her when she needed it most. I was there at the right time, and the imitation was good enough, I guess. But when we were together again, we knew we weren't the same two people any more. One of the sources of her strength, Sid, maybe the key source, is that she had a strongly developed sense of the ludicrous. In her blackest moments, she gets a hearty, healing reaction to absurdity. And she was the one who made the opening when we were both trying to break it up, in such a way we could both save face and not hurt each other. Across a table she gave me a mocking and wonderful look out of those huge dark brown eyes and said, 'Darling, what were the names of those two types who went to Acapulco? You'd think we'd at least hear from them once in a while. The last I heard they were going to get married, but somehow I never quite believed it. Did you?' It was a masterful escape, Sid, for both of us, and out of that special kind of wild wisdom she has, she provided it. Yes, we parted friends. And it's too easy to look at it, perhaps, as one of those ordinary little affairs that pop up like out of a toaster every time any movie is made, and get chilled out when it's over. But it wasn't like that, Sid. She marked me. You see, I fell in love with the Jenny Bowman that was trying to hide from a world that hadn't been using her very well. And when she stopped trying to hide, that woman was gone, the one I loved. But it is a real and valuable memory and I don't have many of those, and I am not going to mess it up by getting back into her life—or allowing her back into mine—in any way, shape or form. I married Joyce on the rebound from Jenny Bowman. And when Joyce rolled her car into the sea, Jenny was singing in Chicago. She flew out to the funeral. That was the only time I have seen her since. And she didn't say a word then. She just hugged me very hard for about three seconds, and looked at me and went away, and that meant a hell of a lot more than anything anyone else did during that whole horrible week. She has a capacity for friendship. I'm probably boring you with too much of all this, Sid, but what I want to get across is that it wasn't trivial. And it isn't . . . usable. If you've taken me on because you think I can talk her into something easier than some of your other boys, then you made a bad guess."

Wegler was silent for three full minutes, swiveled around,

looking out his windows. He turned back slowly. "It is a warm and touching story and again, Jason, you force me to say that I value you for your integrity. I value you highly. It hurts me to have to use people in the ways I have to use them. It makes me feel shabby, believe me."

"But I tell you I . . ."

Wegler raised a hand. "Please. Let me pick one remark out of your fine account, Jason. 'But I do know I helped her when she needed it most.' It does you credit. It is an honorable way to feel. She came to you in your hour of heartbreak. Can you do less for her? If she needs you now?"

"What are you getting at?"

"I can assume, can I not, that when you and Jenny were in love, you did not keep important secrets from each other?"

"I kept none from her. I can't vouch for her, of course."

"But she told you she had a child?"

"Whatever she told me, Sid, was in confidence."

"I see that she did tell you. A few of us, a very few of us, believe me, in the industry know about this. She was a valuable property even then, you understand. Thirteen years ago. That's how old the boy is now. We hushed it up perfectly. An old scandal, Jason. Dead and buried you would say. But a boy lives. He grows. Her only issue. And the years add importance to such a thing." Suddenly he slapped the script so loudly that Jason Brown jumped. "Do you think she can do this part?"

"Y-Yes."

"Do you think she should do this part?"

"Yes, I do, but . . ."

"Let me finish. Please. In all these years of tours, she has never entered England. Why not? The boy is there. His father is there. Old wounds. Jenny Bowman is just beginning a tour. That is her business. We keep her on a sustaining contract, small money, plux X dollars per picture plus percentage, and a minimum of one every two years. She owes us this picture. We want her for it. The arrangement was that she would come back here after the tour and we would get into it. George Kogan arranged this tour. Paris, Brussels, Berlin, Rome, Israel. Presenting Jenny Bowman. Fine. A month ago I heard a rumor she would open the tour in London. I was astonished, Jason. I was apprehensive. To ease my mind I called certain contacts in New York. I thought that perhaps it was some inescapable booking arrangement. But no. I found that the London engagement was at the *in-*

sistence of Jenny Bowman. And I found that she has been more than normally difficult of late. Moody. Too gay or too depressed. I am a pessimistic man, Jason. If there is any way for things to go wrong, they very probably will. It is the rule I follow. Suppose, in her emotional state, she wants to see the boy, and the boy's father after all these years. The British press is merciless. It is savage. It rends and destroys. It could destroy her. Would you say she is in potential trouble, Jason Brown?"

"Yes. But . . ."

"It is a nervous habit with you, Jason, to say yes and then say but. There is affection between you. She trusts you. And you know no good can come of stirring up something which happened over thirteen years ago. She is vulnerable now. With you to steady her, and the script to remind her of what she might lose . . ."

"And what the studio might lose, Sid."

"Careers have survived strange things, but thus far no one has tested the survival aspects of public knowledge of a bastard child."

"But the father adopted him, didn't he?"

"It would be placed in the worst possible light by the press."

Jason thought for a moment. "So you hired me on the remote chance I might be able to yank your chestnuts out of the fire, Sid. If I can, it is cheap insurance. You've been complimenting me on my integrity. Don't you think I have too much integrity to use an old and valued relationship like that, to go meddle in her life to save the studio a property?"

Wegler shrugged and smiled. "Jason, I could try to be subtle with you, but you have been in the business too long. This is a simple thing, is it not? You have been hired to work on a script. There is a way I want you to work on that script. You can refuse. There is a clause in the contract covering such eventualities, and it is covered in the studio agreement with the Screenwriters' Guild."

The trap had snapped so loudly Jason was startled by the sound of the sharp teeth. He saw himself unemployed and virtually unemployable. He looked blankly at Sidney Wegler and said hollowly, "Why you son of a bitch!"

Wegler shook his head sadly. "As I told you, things like this make me feel shabby. This is Friday. She opens in London Sunday night. Transportation is being arranged for you,

Jason. All expenses of course. Our man in London is Tommy Bird. Use him, but don't trust him. I would go myself, but of course Jenny despises me. A word of advice, Jason. Think of it as something you are doing for her. It will make you much happier."

"Does Jenny know I'm coming?"

"Be a surprise."

Now, on the jet six miles above the black Atlantic, Jason Brown knew he most certainly would be a surprise to Jenny Bowman. And he vowed that he would take Wegler's advice at its face value. Do it for Jenny. And if what seemed best for Jenny Bowman seemed to run counter to what was best for Sidney Wegler, then no one need ever know in what gentle direction he had urged her, if indeed he could exert any influence over her at all. Jenny Bowman, with the bit in her teeth, was a fearsome thing indeed.

He thought of her and felt a little residual quiver of old longing in the pit of his stomach. He remembered what a friend had said of her once. He said Jenny had yare. The word had needed much explanation. It is something a boat has when it turns out to have that little indefinable something the marine architects never built into it. A special rakish style to its buoyancy, that wondrous hell-with-you flavor that the very true and very special boats have.

The handsome stewardess brought him his third drink and gave him the menu for the Air France midnight snack. Something bland, he thought. Traditional offering to the sneaky Goddess of Ulcer. She had not made herself apparent in some time, but he had the dreary expectation that this trip would bring her out of hiding.

(In Acapulco, on the morning beach, they had eaten the hot boiled shrimp and stuffed the shells into the sand, drunk the icy Dos Equis, swum, touched, smiled, looked deep into each others eyes, then hurried to the little rented car to clatter up the long hill to the cabana at the Americana, and she had laughed aloud on the way up, at joy anticipated, at the good tastes of food and heat and love.)

two

TIME MOVED FIVE HOURS and the clock moved ten, and Jason
Brown smiled a crinkled good-by at the stewardess and came
down the boarding steps, fusty with sleep, his legs uncertain
with stiffness, light topcoat slung over one shoulder, a rather
shapeless felt hat on the back of his head. He came down
to a welcome solidity of concrete, a misty, watery sunshine,
the guile and calculated confusions of France, mildly cursing
the efficiency of Wegler's people who had arranged this trip.
He found the area for passengers in transit, not subject to
French customs, recovered his single suitcase, found his reservations on the London shuttle flight in order, checked his
bag through and had forty minutes to kill. He killed it with
some extraordinarily bad coffee, with exercising an impla-
cable resistance against all the efforts—from the exceptionally
clever to the clumsily grotesque—of the French to remove
from his person any available number of dollars, and with
composing and sending a cable to Bonny, styled to make her
laugh. At four years old she seemed far more willing to
accept the knowledge of having an aunt instead of a mother
than she was to comprehend that all the daddies seemed to
go off to work except hers. He imagined it would please her
to be able to tell her small friends that now, for a change,
as a special bonus added to the three weeks of his having
gone to the studio each working day, her daddy was on a
business trip.

Tommy Bird met the London plane. He was a pouched,
balding, fidgety man with tan, nervous eyes, a man a little
too elegantly dressed, a man whose eyes would wander to
look at something off behind you when he was talking most
earnestly. He helped Jason Brown through the swift, grave
politenesses of customs and led him off to a shiny gray
Humber driven by one of his younger associates in the London office.

Tommy Bird was one of the immutable characteristics of
a very volatile industry. The arranger—the meeter and

16

greeter, the local promotion man, the beater of many drums, adjusting his beat to the relative importance of the mission. Jason sensed that, as a writer, he was being given a very muted drumbeat, but the essence of the art was to make the recipient feel that mountains were being moved in his honor.

"Got you in the Dorchester, Mr. Brown. Made sure they'll do right by you, room and service and all. Good location. Park Lane. Here's a card with the office numbers. Mount Street. Not too far from you. Anything you want, anything at all, you just pick up the phone and we'll bust a leg to see you get it."

"I suppose you people have been busy with Jenny Bowman?"

"Actually, no. I mean this concert tour thing is separate. Not that we aren't willing and anxious, you understand. A great star. But she's got her own team along, of course. You here to see her?"

"Didn't they tell you?"

"Out in the field, what you get used to, they don't tell you a thing."

"Just to check over some portions of a script with her."

"Something about Dawn?"

"The Longest Dawn."

"That's it. I remember a thing in the *Reporter*. That's what she does next for us."

Jason Brown looked out the window at the nondescript jumble of the southern part of the city. "Things look a little different," he said.

"When were you here last?"

"Almost five years ago."

"It's jumping. Turnpikes, buildings going up, neon, teen-age gangs, race riots. Civilization finally got here, Jason. Okay if I call you Jason?"

"Please do, Tommy."

"You want I should get hold of Jenny's manager and set anything up for you, Jason?"

"No thanks. I know George Kogan. I can manage."

"She opens a charity thing at the Palladium tonight."

"Yes, I know."

"They could have sold the house three times. And try to get a ticket to the opening, the regular opening. Honest to God, Jason, the years go by and that broad just gets more tremendous. Her and the people, like some big love feast.

Over thirty years in the business I've got, and she hits that first note and it's like ice water running down my back. Jolie used to do that to me, too. She's the most since him. The stateside end of this tour has been a smash, hey?"

"S.R.O. from one end of the country to the other."

"What a property!" Tommy Bird said with a wistful sigh.

As soon as he was checked into the Dorchester, he thanked Tommy Bird and his young associate and sent them on their way. He had forgotten the pleasure of being checked in by hotel people who seemed to take a genuine pleasure in serving him and making him welcome. He refused assistance in unpacking. The tall windows of his sedate room looked out across Hyde Park. He unpacked, took a hot bath, put on a dark suit suitable for the evening, sent the suit he had traveled in to be pressed, and went down and had a late and rather heavy lunch in a quiet corner of a big hushed dining room. He knew there was no point in trying to establish contact with Jenny prior to a performance.

After the leisurely lunch, he put on his topcoat as protection against the increasing chill of the afternoon, and took a long walk through the relative emptiness of the West End on a Sunday afternoon, Piccadilly, Bond Street, St. James Square, Regent Street. London gave him a feeling of pleasant anonymity, of a measured and timeless courtesy, a feeling that if he had been able to walk on his hands, he would attract very little additional attention. It is, he thought, an older and more complex culture, larded with a certain smugness, shot through with little social nuances and distinctions we never catch, vastly more tolerant of eccentricity. A society of contradictions as strange as our own. They bowdlerize their novels, yet print daily papers exploiting the more feral and rancid aspects of sex with a smirking boldness unknown in all the rest of the western world. And he could guess what they would do to Jenny Bowman, given the slightest opening. She thought herself inured to a bad press. She had earned one from time to time. And the bigger you get, the smaller the incident required. But she would be utterly, incredulously vulnerable to what the British press would do to her.

And this, he thought sourly, would be the result of a certain quality of decency over thirteen years ago. If Wegler had anything to do with it at that time, he could imagine the pressure on Jenny to fly to Sweden or Japan and have the pregnancy terminated. Jenny Bowman, he decided, had never been in the habit of making small mistakes. Her errors were as vast as her talents.

He struck west from Regent Street, got lost once, and then came out on Argyll Street not far from the Palladium. It was just dusk and the marquee lights had not been turned on, but he could read her name. Jenny Bowman. A recognition, as valid in Cairo as in Buenos Aires. It was a name that picked up a little corner of everyone's mind and riffled that stack of memories. And for everyone they were good memories. Maybe that was the key to her. Dozens of journeyman movies and a few, a very few great ones, but who has ever had many of those? And those songs she had made her own, had stamped so permanently and indelibly with her personality and the cadence and tone and heart of her that any other singer attacking them sounded at once imitative, shallow and apologetic.

Jason Brown stepped out of the cool wind on Argyll Street to relight his pipe and heard the faint music from inside, a big band coming down solid and hard on "When You're Smiling." The music broke off and, after a hesitation, took it again from the top. He grinned and thought of George Kogan in there, man of all talents, working hard with the leader, doing the final smoothing of the beat and tempo, while in some hotel suite Jenny would be stretched out, a little more pallid than usual, staring a hole through the ceiling as she ran all the lyrics through her mind and fretted, as she always did, about her voice.

He turned away. After two blocks he remembered the name of an East Indian place where he and Joyce had eaten a curry so savage the tears had run down their cheeks. He hailed a cab. The driver knew the place and said it was still open. As soon as he walked in, Jason Brown knew it was a mistake. The memories were too strong, the years too mercilessly swift. But he stayed and ate, as though it were a penance. This memory—all memories of Joyce were linked to Jenny Bowman. One love conditions you for the next. Somehow, with Jenny, he had become hooked on that feeling of simulated strength, the needed man syndrome. And, in rebound from Jenny when she was whole again, he had almost consciously sought a woman who would need him. Joyce had been lovely, sensitive, intelligent, ardent, adoring, amusing. And she had been a drunk. What greater need? And in the first genuine binge after Bonny was born, she had failed to make that curve south of San Clemente.

God only knew where she was headed. The police following her said nobody could have made it at a hundred miles an hour. But almost five years ago they had been at that corner table, and she was three months pregnant, six months sober, and she had been fruitful, luminous, loving, the shade of her dress turning her eyes to pure lavender.

He walked again and it was almost eleven when he reached the Palladium. The big cars were waiting, the chauffeurs in small groups, smoking and talking. There were flocks of taxis and London policemen waiting to take care of the mass exodus. When he was fifty feet away, he heard that sudden explosion of sound which meant she had finished a number. It was a rushing, roaring sound and it seemed to have, as always, a depth of tone and a resonance other entertainers seldom called forth. The great animal called Audience bayed with all its thousands of throats and made the back of his neck and the backs of his hands tingle. He found the stage door. He rattled the latch and the commissionaire opened it a half foot and looked out at him dubious and questioning, a stately old gentleman of vast dignity.

"Miss Bowman's party," he said and handed the man his card.

"Please wait one moment, sir." The door closed, and two minutes later it swung open. "Down this corridor, sir. Then to your right. Watch the steps. Mr. Kogan is there in the wings."

"How many encores?"

"This, I believe, would be the seventh, sir. They completely refuse to let her leave stage."

"They never do," he said, and he walked toward the sound of that marvelously flexible and powerful voice. He knew there would be an eighth encore, because this time she was turning the pressure down with a ballad, "Almost Like Being in Love," done in a throaty yet limpid and effortless style.

There were three people in the wings, in silhouette against the bright spot that shone on the dark hair and the glittering gown of Jenny Bowman as she sang to the people, turning their hearts over. He knew the silhouettes of George Kogan and Ida Mulligan, her dresser and companion. When he came up behind them he saw that the third one was a sandy-haired young man he did not know.

When he touched George on the shoulder, George swiveled

around, looked blankly at him, gave him a crushing hand-shake and said in a tense husky whisper, "She's great! My God, she's great!" He turned back. Ida stepped to him, hugged him hard, kissed his cheek.

"George will remember to say hello a little later," she whispered. "For me, hello Jase. We're really glad to see you."

At the last skilled note the great roar came again. George Kogan jumped up and down and banged Jason on the shoulder with his fist. "London restraint!" he yelled. "British reserve! Listen to 'em! Just listen to 'em!"

Jenny swooped up an armful of bouquets, bowed and bowed, her smile brilliant, and the curtain came down and she came swiftly toward them in that remembered walk. It was a dancer's walk, with a dancer's grace, but it had a small flavor of gamin about it, as though at any moment she could walk a fence, play stickball, imitate a punchy fighter. She came toward them with the tension of rapport in her face, that listening look. She could not belong to them in any sense until it was ended, and she stopped be-longing to the audience. Jason moved back into the shadows. The heavy curtain smothered some of the sound but it kept coming in great waves. She thrust the bouquets into the arms of the sandy young man and said, "Open a store, Gabe."

The young man revealed his calling by dumping the flow-ers into Ida's arms, and touching Jenny's hair very swiftly and deftly, tucking stray strands into place.

"A blast!" George said. "You better talk them down, or we can have breakfast sent in."

"Shall try," she said and went back out, more slowly, and positioned herself at the microphone, waited a few moments, then nodded toward the far wings. As the curtain went up the sound of the audience strengthened, smashing against the stage in the way that made Jason Brown think of heavy surf. She held her hands up, palms out, and slowly she si-lenced them. Jason marveled at how small she seemed out there, how small and yet how indomitable.

In a totally conversational tone of voice she said, "You are wonderful people, and I love you every one, and I would love to stand here and sing to you all night long." The ap-plause and shouts started but she silenced them again. "But my manager is standing back there with his whip and the leg irons, and he says this is absolutely the last one. This a warm and wonderful welcome to London. I'll never forget you." She aimed a finger at the band leader, like pointing a pistol. "Now here we go!" The band hit the intro to her arrangement of "Chicago." She moved, keying herself to the beat and the brass, and went into it, taking the tempo and seeming to lift it, giving herself with all the little turns and struttings of her effort, yet making it all seem without effort, making it seem a total enjoyment. Jason Brown felt it take him as completely as it was taking the big audience, shallowing his breath, running his blood faster. It was the essence of professionalism, but it was also something more, something you could never quite put your finger on. It was the same thing, perhaps, which made her sing to friends with all the skill and care and effort she would give to a great audience. It was her communication, her projection of her spirit and her love.

(Once, after the pool lights were off at the Americana, and it was a rare moonlight, they had swum then sat close on the low board, and she had sung "Stormy Weather" for him, muting all the power of that voice down to a small and wondrous clarity of tone, audible only to him, her pale strong throat throbbing in the silver fall of tropic moonlight, making of that song a love offering so sweet the tears in his eyes had blurred the image of her.)

Again came the great crashing sound of applause. She gathered up more of the flowers. She bowed and smiled and bowed. George Kogan signaled the stage man and the curtain came down, and George walked out to her. He grabbed her and hugged her, full of excitement. "Great! Great! Great! Great!" he said. "You're great!"

She stood there, barely aware of him, head tilted, wearing her listening look. Jason Brown heard the applause finally begin to diminish, and he saw her give a small nod. Now she could let the long and exhausting contact with them fade, and she could come back to herself, to the private Jenny Bowman. The hairdresser was picking up more flowers. Jenny handed the ones she held to George, and he said, "Listen to them, they're going out of their skins!"

She started toward the corner of the stage and Jason Brown moved to block her way. She stared at him absently almost irritably and her face changed. "Brownie!" she said, all a sudden gladness. She squeezed him and kissed him and shook her head marvelingly. "I see you and know how much I've missed you."

"You were really something tonight, Jenny dear."

"Wasn't I just?" she said with a mockery unlike her, tiredness in her face and an obscure look of anger. "Come along," she said, and moved by him, ignoring the robe Ida held out for her. The four of them followed her back through the vast and shadowy dinginess of the backstage areas, all the big flats and dust, the dangling webs of heavy cables and ropes. Someone on one of the overhead catwalks, stagehand or electrician, called down, "Great show, Jenny!"

She glanced up and acknowledged with a wave.

"Twenty songs and eight encores," George said. "Admit it, darling. There's nothing wrong with that voice."

She did not answer him. As some of the backstage people moved toward her, George quickened his stride and deftly waved them off, saying to Jenny, "Darling, with all honesty and sincerity, you were magnificent."

They reached the dressing room corridor where Jason had been before, and as Jenny and Ida and the hairdresser continued on to the dressing room, George stopped and turned to the commissionaire and beckoned and said, "Hey, you—Chief!" Jason stood by, waiting for a chance to speak to George.

"Yes sir?"

"No one gets by here. Understand? No one."

"No one. Yes sir."

The people were already gathering, moving down the corridor and the commissionaire hastened to block their way. Jason saw two photographers in the group, one of them saying, "Let me through. Let me through. Press. One side, please."

George Kogan said with a smiling, easy affability, "I'm sorry, boys. You'll have to settle for what you've got."

"But you promised one in the dressing room."

"I'm sorry."

Jason saw the orchestra leader push through the group and George moved to meet him and intercept him, saying, "Larry, Jenny asked me to . . ."

"Wasn't she great!" the orchestra leader said.

"Superb. Listen, she asked me to tell you she's a little tired now . . ." He turned to the insistent photographers and said with a trace of irritation, "Boys, I told you I'm sorry."

A woman with a large bouquet was trying to edge past the commissionaire. She said, "Mr. Kogan! This man apparently doesn't realize. I'm Mrs. Glynne. You remember me. I'm chairman of the committee."

George stepped to her and gently took the flowers. "May I?"

"But I wanted to thank her. In the name of the Children's Fund. Really, more than ten thousand pounds . . ."

"Just thirty seconds of her time," the orchestra leader said, and then George, Mrs. Glynne, the photographers and the orchestra leader were all talking at the same time, as the commissionaire kept all the others back, saying "Sorry, madam. Sorry, sir."

Jason Brown leaned against the corridor wall near the dressing room and watched George Kogan handle the confusion expertly, placating them, thanking them in the name of Jenny Bowman, telling them she had given so much of herself to that splendid audience she was exhausted. In a little while the confusion dwindled as Larry, Mrs. Glynne and the photographers gave up and turned away. When it was apparent the commissionaire could handle it, George came slowly toward Jason Brown. He looked wearied and thoughtful, and he shook hands again and said, "Nice to see you, Jase." Kogan was a man of great enthusiasms and a high order of organizational skill, but at this moment he looked subdued. "What are you doing over here?"

"I came over to see Jenny."

George was immediately alert. "Now that seems interesting. And what would you come over here to see her about, Jase?"

"Check over the script with her, when she has a chance."

Kogan pursued his lips. "Well, now! I'm reputed to be her manager, and little things like this come through me, don't they? Doesn't the studio like to set up these little things properly? Wouldn't it have been common courtesy to let us know? And isn't this a little bit out of your normal line of work?"

Jason shrugged. "I'm on the script, George. Just say it was sort of spur of the moment. You know. Run over and check a couple of things out with Jenny."

George nodded. "Spur of the moment. I like that. Sid Wegler never did anything on impulse in his whole life, pal."

Jason sighed. "Okay, okay. I've never been any damned good at conspiracy. Wegler added two and two, and he got a little nervous. Believe me, George, I didn't want to come over, but I got mousetrapped. Maybe Wegler thinks I can be a steadying influence or something. Let me ask you this way, George. Is there any cause for alarm?"

"You have to answer a question first, Brown. Whose side are you on?"

Jason thought it over. "You get a compound answer. I will go through the motions for Wegler. But basically I'm on Jenny's side. You should know that."

"I make a career out of suspicion. You're right. I should know that. Yes, Jase, we have some cause for alarm. She's been moody, blue, defiant, unpredictable. I had to book us into London or she would have blown the whole tour. She said it and meant it."

"What is she after?"

"I don't think she knows."

"Has she made contact?"

"She's been trying ever since the moment we got here. I've tried to tell her it is potentially a very damaging situation, but she's at the state where she doesn't seem to give a damn. If you can make her realize that, I'm going to be grateful to Sid Wegler for the first time in my life." He hesitated. "You know how shrewd she is. She senses things. I better tell her I knew somebody was coming and forgot to tell her. It will set better. Come on, let's go on in."

"Should I wait and see her later?"

"She'll want to see you now." He reached to rap on the dressing room door and turned, frowning. "I wasn't with her then. My tour of duty is ten years so far. But Ida was. Anyway, I never heard any mention of Wegler. And damned few people know."

"He was in on it, from the studio end. He helped hush it up."

George nodded. "I can understand more why she hates the guy. He wouldn't have the slightest idea of what it meant to her."

"And he probably exerted the deciding pressure that made her give up the child. She hinted as much to me."

"Sometimes," George said, "it's a very cruddy profession." He gave a single rap on the door and opened it and went in, Jason following him. It was a sizable dressing room. Jenny sat at the dressing table, wearing a robe. The hairdresser was pouring Jenny a drink.

Jenny turned and said, "Brownie, you look great. And it's been too long. George, what am I stuck with?"

George tossed Mrs. Glynne's bouquet into a chair and said, "Absolutely nothing. You don't have to see anyone."

"You are a dear man," she said.

George roamed over and parted the curtains and looked out the window, back toward the stage door. "It's started to rain hard," he said wonderingly, "and there must be five hundred of them milling around out there. London loves you, sweetie."

"Oh sure," she said. She sipped her drink, made a grimace of pain and rubbed the side of her face and throat. The hairdresser moved in behind her and began combing and fixing her hair.

"Why don't you lie down?" Ida Mulligan said. "You'll get in a state."

"I'm in a state. Make the call again."

Ida shrugged and picked up the phone, placed the call. George poured a drink for himself and one for Jason and took Jason's over to him. Jason could sense the tension in the room.

"Doctor Donne, please," Ida said into the phone. Jenny turned her head sharply and stared at Ida, her expression tense and expectant. After a pause, Ida shook her head at Jenny and she relaxed. "Then when do you expect him? . . . Yes, it's Miss Bowman again." Jenny got up quickly and began to pace. The hairdresser stood waiting patiently for her by the bench, comb in hand. "Well, *can* he be reached? . . . Yes, it is an emergency. Thank you. I'll wait. What's that? Well, when you do, have him call Miss Bowman. Thank you." She hung up. "He'll call," she said.

"Where is he?" Jenny demanded.

"In the country."

"Call the country!"

"They're calling the country."

George said, "Larry was wondering about . . ."

Jenny whirled on him and said, "I tell you I'm losing my voice!"

"So we notice," Ida said quietly.

"And I want a doctor!"

"We've got the name of a doctor," Ida said. "Doctor Rudolph Lessing."

"Call him," George said.

"But I want Doctor Donne, dammit!"

Jason saw George glance at Ida in the silence. Jason could

feel the tension and he suspected the three of them had forgotten his presence.

Ida said, "But maybe he doesn't want to see you."

Jenny glowered at her. "He's a doctor, isn't he? He's got to see me. It's medical ethics, isn't it?" She was standing still, and the hairdresser moved to stand behind her and work on her hair, fluffing it with great deftness, and she seemed totally unaware of him.

George moved close to her and took her hand. "Jenny, can I advise you as a friend? Why don't you get dressed and we get the hell out of here, go get something to eat someplace. Jenny darling, you've been losing your voice for twenty years and you still haven't lost it. But this time it's different? So okay, it's different. Then you need a doctor. By all means, let's get a doctor. The best in London. And if he's not enough, we'll fly Bidderman from the coast. But please, I beg you, leave David Donne alone."

She pulled her hand away and asked quietly, "Is that the advice?"

"That's the advice."

The phone rang. Ida answered it. Jenny turned and watched her, very tense. When Ida held the phone out toward George, Jenny's shoulders sagged. George took it and said, "Speaking. Yeh, sure." He turned to Jenny. "First cut on the new album is finished. You want to hear it tomorrow?"

"Not tomorrow," Jenny said in a dull voice.

"They'll arrange it at our convenience."

"Not tomorrow."

George spoke into the phone. "We'll have to work it in. I'll call you. Okay? Good. Fine." As he hung up the phone rang immediately. He picked it up. "Hello? Yes. Hold on." With a tired and rueful smile he held the phone out, handed it to Jenny. "Your doctor."

Jason could sense Jenny's nervousness as she took the phone, and the effort she was making to hide it. "David, how are you? Yes, a long time. Too long. . . . Well, I've been combing the hills for you. . . . As a matter of fact, not too well . . . I can't explain over the phone . . . No, not tomorrow, tonight . . . No, I really can't tomorrow. The first cut on a new album is ready and I have a listening session and a run-through. . . ." George gave Jason a sardonic glance. "I know, I know, I'm sure you have, but honestly, David . . . let's not be reasonable, let's be unreason-

able. . . ." She began to smile. "Fine—where are you?
. . . No, I'd rather come to you. Wimpole Street? Fifteen or
twenty minutes? I'll see you then. Good-by, David."

She hung up, still smiling and turned to George and said,
"I'll need Tom and the car."

"It's done."

She turned to Jason, her face young and lovely again, her
big brown eyes shining, her smile a little more soft than
theatrical. "Brownie, dear, I want to talk to you about a
thousand things. We'll have a chance. You'll be around?"

"Sure."

She turned back toward George and Ida, her tone ex-
planatory, "You know, when you're really worried, a
doctor you have real confidence in is . . ."

"Sure, Jenny," Ida said. "We know."

"Well . . . let's roll the wagons!" she said with a burst of
electric energy and good cheer. "Let's move!" The hairdresser fixed a final curl. Ida reached and took a slip and a
dress from their hangers. George nodded at Jason, and Jason
followed him out of the dressing room.

"I guess it has begun," George said.

"Seems as if."

"I hope the good doctor has a lot more sense than he had
thirteen years ago," George said dispiritedly. "Let me tell
Tom to stand by, then suppose you come on back to the
hotel with me and we'll hold hands and cry."

three

THE BOWMAN TEAM was staying at the Park Lane, not far from Jason's hotel. A small paneled grillroom was still open. Jason and George sat in a low corner booth padded in black leather, and when their drinks were served, Kogan rubbed tired eyes and said, "It could be such a smooth operation, Jase. Aside from Jenny, there's the traveling package, and we all know our jobs. Herm Rice on music, musicians, arrangements. Jorgensen on sets and lighting. Herm and Jorgy are over in Paris getting it set up for us over there. Hope we make it. Gabe, the hairdresser. Lois Marney on secretarial, tickets, bookkeeping, reservations, odds and ends. She'll be down in a couple of minutes. It's a good team, Jase, believe me. Trial by fire, and you get a good team. And loyal. Everybody is loyal. Like Ida, my God, eighteen years. So it isn't so good to watch her chew herself up, but what can you do?"

"Wait and see, I guess. And try to help."

"And pray a little. Here comes Lois."

They both slid out of the booth and stood up. George introduced them. Lois Marney seemed to be about thirty, a tall blonde woman in a gray wool suit of rather severe tailoring, a white blouse with a nest of ruffles at her throat. Her hand was cool and dry in his. She wore her blonde hair short, combed to glossiness, a diagonal slant of bangs across her forehead. Her hair was curled around behind her ears, brought forward, giving her a look of sophistication and, somehow, an innocence and credulity. It was an oval face, fine-textured, the brows straight and rather heavy over light gray eyes, the mouth level and self-contained. She carried a flat purse and a red manila envelope. She slid into the semicircular booth and they sat on either side of her, Jason at her left.

"Rouse you out of the sack?" George asked.

"Oh sure! I finished a long letter to those nuts in Brussels, wherein you reassure them about everything." She started to untie the folder. "If you could read it over and sign it . . ."

George put his hand on hers and stopped her. "I phoned you to come down social, Lois dear. Business as usual tomorrow. Okay?"

"If I can catch you in orbit tomorrow. How did it go?"

"She was a hundred and ten percent fabulous, believe me. She cut them off at eight encores, and she could have gone a dozen easy. And when she left, in the rain, it took cops to get her through the crush and into the limousine. But . . . she got in touch with him, and that's where she is right now."

Lois Marney stiffened and gave a quick glance at Jason Brown.

George saw it and said, "Down, girl. Jase is an old friend, and a trusted friend. Consider him part of the group."

Lois turned and stared at Jason. She bit her underlip, her head slightly tilted. "Would Jenny call you Brownie?"

"She's the only one who does."

Lois smiled at him and it was a warmer smile than he had anticipated. "Now I know who you are. We get so darned accustomed to keeping up our guard."

"Except for Gabe, who doesn't really count," George said, "Lois is the junior member of the team. Two and a half years."

Lois turned to George. "She went to see him?"

"She put it on a medical basis. She went off to have him stare down her throat. Naturally, she's losing her voice. I don't know what she wants. I don't know how he'll react. Hell, she doesn't know how she will react. But she had to see him. And she wasn't about to take me along."

"Did she seem happy when she left?" Lois asked.

"Nervous," George said. "Excited. Tensed up. And so am I. Lois dear, you can usually eat anything at any time. How about the roast beef sandwich that's coming for me? My stomach is in knots. Stay and keep Jase company. Sorry, Jase. See you tomorrow. Look, you can tell Lois the Wegler thing, and why. Honey, I'll take this folder along and read your letter and sign it and leave it in your box in the morning."

"I'll eat your sandwich, George. Good night."

He waved a weary arm and trudged away.

"Strange, isn't it?" Lois said. "She's a grown woman. But

we get this . . . savage protective feeling about her. I guess we just don't want her to be hurt. She's such a wonderful person."

"I think it's because we sense how especially vulnerable she is, Lois. Maybe it goes with the talent. I don't know. But her pendulum swings a little further than yours and mine. A greater capacity for joy, perhaps. Certainly a greater capacity to feel pain and hurt and despair."

She looked intently at him and nodded. "More range, sort of. Yes. You know how she is. She gets very rough with us, with all of us. And we're not door mat types, any of us. But then she is so horrified at herself, we sort of comfort her. There isn't a warmer person anywhere. You can't say she has a child's emotions. They're too deep and strong for that. And there are the professional disciplines, of course. She has, I think, a child's lack of control over a stronge woman's emotions. But I'm not in any sense trying to cut her up, Mr. Brown."

"Jase, please."

"Jase. Jason. I'd rather call you Jason, if that's all right."

"I'd like it better, I guess."

The sandwiches and coffee came. She began to eat with obvious relish. "She was in love with you once upon a time, Jason."

"We were in love. We thought we were in love."

"You believed it, didn't you?"

"Yes."

"What can there be, beyond believing it?"

"It was exactly the right time for us, when she was not herself and I was not myself, and the two people we happened to be—they fell in love. But then those two people ceased to exist."

"That must happen oftener than people know," she said with a pretty thoughtfulness. "I guess that happened to me. But maybe he wasn't really not himself. I just looked at him and saw somebody else. But I married the guy. And it was a disaster. Five years of disaster. We got a divorce three years ago."

"If I'd married Jenny, it would have turned into a disaster, sooner or later."

"Like the other two marriages? No, not like that. I think . . . no matter what . . . you two would have been kinder to each other."

"I came along between those two marriages."

"She's still fond of you, Jason."

"I'm glad."

"I have the feeling she's going to need her friends."

"I'll be able to stay around for a while."

She finished the last of the sandwich, touched the napkin to her lips and gave him an uneasy, sidelong glance. "I'm wondering right now how much I can trust you."

"It won't do any good for me to tell you that you can. Let me tell you the background on why I'm here."

She listened intently to his story of how Wegler had trapped him and was using him. "It's sort of a . . . feline trick, isn't it?" she said. "But the main idea is to keep Jenny from . . . being foolish. Of course, he's thinking of the damned picture and we're thinking of Jenny as a person, so it adds up to the same thing."

"You have a very practical mind, Lois."

She studied him for a few moments and nodded. "I guess I'll trust you. I'll tell you what's bothering me, has been bothering me. After this London thing first came up, everybody started getting tense. And I didn't know why. I went to George and demanded to know what was going on. He wouldn't tell me, and I said I didn't care to work in that kind of an atmosphere, and finally he pledged me to secrecy and told me. But he didn't embellish it any. Just the cold facts. Now I think I know Jenny Bowman. I think I know her pretty well, as a matter of fact. And I cannot imagine her giving up her own child. That's what floors me every time I think of this mess. Jason, could you please help me understand how such a thing could be?"

"I think I can. I hope I can. But it will take a little time and these people seem to want to close this place up."

"Oh, of course. Don't pay, Jason. They have my signature on record here."

"Let's let Mr. Wegler take care of it."

"Oh, of course he should. It's more fitting, isn't it?"

As she slid along the booth and stood up, he became more aware of her figure and the way she handled herself. She had a strong body under the fitted gray suit, a round firm breadth of hip, long round legs, straight back, a heaviness of breast above a slim flat waist. She handled herself with a slowness and a care that made her seem slightly, enchantingly awkward.

They went into the empty and rather cheerless lobby. They looked outside and it had begun to rain again. She smiled at him and he thought he detected a slight flush as she said, "I guess I better compromise you, Jason. Somebody gave us all some sort of extra-fabulous Scotch, and they might even send us up some ice, complete with slightly pained expression."

Her room was on the third floor. As they walked down the corridor, she said, "Jenny is in a suite back there with Ida, and George is across the corridor from them." She handed him her key and he unlocked her door. It was a larger room than his. She'd had a table brought in and was using it as a desk. There was a portable electric typewriter, two portable files, a stack of correspondence.

"Welcome to the office," she said. "Office, travel bureau, advertising agency, ticket office and wailing wall." She got the Scotch out of the closet, ordered up ice, and made casual talk about her work until the ice had come and he had fixed their drinks. He stretched out on a chaise and she sat a few feet away in an armchair.

"Better than the lobby," he said.

"You overwhelm me with extravagant compliments. Cheers."

"This is really *very* good stuff," he said.

"Tell me about Jenny."

"All right. I have to take a writer's privileges here. Some she told me. Some I guessed. Some of it I inferred from other things she said. Now imagine Jenny in her twenties. Vulnerable then too, but in a different way. She had been working very hard for a very long time, and she had become, through work and drive and talent, a success. She was known. She was valuable. But there was still a long way to go, and she probably had that feeling of certainty of being right on the edge of all the marvelous things to come. She was working in New York. Suddenly, quite suddenly, her voice began to fail. The people with a big interest in her future got her the best medical attention. But none of them could find anything organic. They talked about anxiety, psychological factors. But Jenny *knew* it had to be something else. She could see all the future going out the window. She was in despair. Then somebody suggested a bright young specialist who was studying and working temporarily at Presbyterian Hospital. David Donne. A most attractive young Englishman. He went into the problem with great care and found something the others had missed. I don't know exactly what he found. It doesn't really matter. Some nerve involvement in the larynx which responded to minor surgery and a period of complete rest, of not using her voice even for speech. She remained in New York during that period, so he could keep her under observation. When she was alone she would get so terrified her voice would never come back, that she would be tempted to try to use it, and then she would hurry to him, because only with him could she hold on to her confidence. She became dependent upon him, emotionally dependent. They fell in love. They had an affair. She became pregnant. I think you can see how it happened to her. Proximity, vulnerability, fear, dependence. His conduct was, of course, unethical. She was a patient. But he was young and lonely and far from home, and this was a lovely, emotional woman. And New York is a city to make both of them more vulnerable. As you can guess from being with her, Jenny hasn't got the typical show biz attitude toward the quick cheap affair. She has to be totally, intensely, emotionally involved."

"Yes. I know."

"So, she learned she was pregnant, and then the waiting time was up, and she had all of her voice back, clear and strong and true. They had engagements lined up for her, and she told the powers that be that she was very sorry, but she was going to have a baby. David Donne's baby. The pressure came down on her from every side. Big pressure. Big money pressure. David Donne was already married, his wife here in England. She resisted the pressure to force her to have an abortion until three months had passed, and then it was too dangerous. She was aghast at the idea of killing it. She would have it and she would keep it and she would raise it. And she refused to make any cover-story marriage.

"They had long months to work on her and on the young doctor. And they had good legal talent to work out the details. Donne went back to England and made full confession to his wife. They had no children, and her health was such it did not appear that they ever would. She forgave him and agreed to the tentative arrangement. The one the lawyers had suggested. Then Donne came back and presented the whole thing to Jenny. An illegitimate child would very probably smash her career. She could not hope to keep it quiet, if she kept the child with her. And would it be good for the child, to be branded in that way? He could legally adopt the child. His wife had agreed. They would love the child and care for it and raise it properly, and it need never know the circumstances of its birth. If she claimed to love the unborn child, how could she deny it such a chance, and force upon it the stigma of illegitimacy? I guess they worked on her in shifts. They finally wore her down. She signed the papers. They hid her away. She gave birth to a boy, and they were smart enough never to let her see it, never to let her hold it in her arms even once, because if they had, she would have tipped over all their applecarts. Part of the agreement was that she would never try to find the boy, never see him again. Can you understand a little better, Lois?"

"Of course," she said softly. "I should have been able to figure it out myself, how it would be."

"She really hurled herself into the career once she came out of hiding. The disappearance was all attributed to the throat operation, and if there were any rumors, I don't remember hearing them. Maybe, in one sense, a lot of her drive during these intervening years has been partially due to compensation. This is what she gave her baby away for. So she had to make it big and good and valid."

"She would have been as good in either case, Jason."

"Would she have worked as hard?"

"Perhaps not. Anyway, what now?"

"I suppose she wants to see the boy."

"Would Doctor Donne permit that?"

"I don't know, Lois. I have no idea what kind of a man he is."

"We did a little checking. We know he's a very successful man. Very. Put it this way. If there was some sort of nose and throat trouble in the royal family and they called in some people for consultation, he would be one of them."

"Fashionable, eh?"

"As well as very good. And being very good is the best fashion of all, I guess."

"How will his wife react, I wonder."

"She died several years ago."

Jason Brown was startled. "Really! Maybe Jenny wants them both."

"Or thinks she does."

A twist of the wind slapped rain against the windows, startling them. She got up and took his glass and fixed him a fresh drink and brought it to him. She went back to the chair with her drink, sat and crossed her long legs, smiled at him with a slight stain of wistfulness. "Even though

George works me like a dog, I was really happy about this tour. I don't know. I guess I've been going a little stale or something. But it isn't the way I thought it would be."

"Things will work out."

"That's so easy to say."

"Dialogue," he said.

"I beg your pardon?"

He smiled. "Excuse me. It slipped out. The artificiality of the breed. The writer has to watch it. He's one step removed from life. So, instead of speaking he finds himself opening his mouth and making bad dialogue, without communication. I even find myself doing it with my daughter. Daddy-Bonny talk, for bad television. So I guess everybody goes stale in his own fashion."

"You're married now?"

"No. I was. My wife died when Bonny was almost a year old. We live with my married sister in Santa Barbara."

She scowled at her drink. "I guess I'm using Jenny as an excuse, really. The thing about staleness, you take it with you. You suddenly find out you've brought it to London. I don't know what it is, really. I run around madly doing a thousand things, and then I have the feeling I've done nothing at all." She looked at him and her gray eyes were very frowning and intent.

"Life is the process of being used, of being satisfyingly used," he said.

Her eyes changed. She looked pale and uncertain. "Are you . . . used that way?" she said in a voice so low it was almost a whisper.

"Once in a rare while in my work. Too seldom. Often with Bonny. Otherwise, no."

She looked away and there was a flavor of strain and awkwardness in the room. "Well," he said too heartily. "Thank you for delicious Scotch and a place out of the rain, but I better be heading back."

She stood up also, smiling politely, saying, "Thanks for telling me about how it must have been for her. I understand now."

They went to the door and he turned toward her. They both started to speak at once, and both stopped. They smiled at each other, and suddenly her smile was crooked and uncertain. Asking himself what the hell he thought he was doing, he reached clumsily at Lois Marney and pulled her into his arms. He kissed her. She felt bulky and resistant in his arms. Her lips were firm and still. He felt that he had blundered into an impossible situation. Then suddenly her arms slid quite shyly around his waist, her mouth turned warm, soft and responsive, he heard her deep shuddering breath, and through some miracle of compliance her body was suddenly smaller, closer, more pliant and useful. He kissed her and held her for a few moments, and let her go at her first stirring toward release. She backed away and looked at him somberly and he was astonished to see her eyes were full of tears.

"A rainy night in London town or something," he said.

"Please don't get all humble and apologetic, Jason. I think I asked for it."

"Then it was a splendid idea."

"Was it? I don't know. I don't know how vulnerable I am any more. I don't know what I want. But I think I know what did it."

"Do you?"

"What we were talking about, directly and indirectly, was loneliness. And I think we made each other aware of our own loneliness."

"But don't cry about it."

She smiled. "I feel sorry for myself on rainy nights. Go home, Jason."

"At the moment, it's an unpleasant suggestion. But valid. If I tried to stay, if you let me stay, I'd talk it to death. It's one of my specialities."

She raised a mocking brow. "Dialogue?"

"Exactly. Good night, Lois."

"Good night, dear Jason." He turned and opened the door. "Jason?" she came to him, put her hands on his cheeks, kissed his mouth with precision, emphasis and a brief and startling hint of passion. "If we ever find another rainy night," she said, "we'll have to find some way to muzzle you." She pushed him gently and firmly into the corridor and closed the door.

Jason Brown stood mildly in the corridor, shaking his head. He put on his topcoat as he walked to the elevators. He put his shapeless hat on the back of his head. He fumbled for his pipe and hummed a tuneless tune.

The rain had slowed to a gentle drizzle, and he walked to the Dorchester. Twenty after two on a Monday morning in London. Though he seldom felt attuned to his environment, at this time he felt particularly unreal. Jenny Bowman had run through his life once before, like an unattended bull-dozer, and when the dust had settled, he was married to Joyce. There I was, he thought, in the room Betty fixed over for me, sweating out the novel, fretting about the anemic bank account, wondering how soon I would have to phone Sandy and needle him to get me a television script, just for walking-around money. And then the past, in the form of Jenny Bowman, reaches out and snags me, yanks me across one continent, drops me on another, and has me kissing a splendidly structured and sturdy blonde secretary the first time I ever see her.

As he prepared for bed, he wondered if Jenny Bowman would ever know, could ever know the inadvertent disruptions she had caused in a thousand lives. The elemental force and persuasion of talent. He turned off the bed light and thought of Jenny Bowman. The eyes wide set, deeply brown, expressive, constantly changing, and all the breadth of the face across the eyes, tapering to the hearty yet vulnerable mouth, and the small and incurably wistful chin.

(They had come in out of the Acapulco sun, and he had been stretched out on the bed reading a script she had brought along, something they wanted her to do, and he had looked up and seen her measuring her waist with a tape measure and asked her exactly what she thought she was doing. She had come to the foot of the bed, looking puzzled and amused. "Brownie, when I am miserable, I get *fat*. And when I'm happy I get *fat*. But how in heck does a girl stay halfway between?" He had suggested that if she was getting too smug, he could beat her once in a while. She could put it in her appointment book and remind him.)

But as he neared sleep, his mind veered to Lois Marney, and he was surprised to find he had so many particularly vivid memories of her. Without realizing he was doing it, he had apparently filed away every tilt of her smooth blonde head, every flicker of expression, every pleasant stretch and curve of the gray wool fabric of her severe suit. "Old goat," he murmured, and went contentedly to sleep.

four

JASON BROWN'S ROOM phone rang at five minutes after nine, and he found it and mumbled into it before he had the slightest idea of where he was, and only a fragmentary notion of who he was.

"You sound like a faulty drain, pal," George Kogan said. "Rise and glow, Jase. She rooted me out, and now she wants you."

"Jenny?"

"Jenny Bowman herself."

"Not the Jenny I remember. Not at this hour."

"Today would seem to be one of those days. She is full of hectic enthusiasm, and she will not talk to anybody except her old buddy Brownie. The show is on the road, so crank yourself up and come over."

Ida opened the door of the suite. She tapped herself on the temple and gestured over her shoulder with her thumb. "In there."

Jenny was propped up in a big bed wearing a quilted yellow robe, a breakfast table across her lap. "Good morning! It's a lovely day. Shut the door, Brownie darling." He shut the door. She held her arms out. He went over to kiss her. There was a toast crumb on her lip. He picked up her napkin and brushed it away and kissed her.

"Always fastidious," she said. "God, it's good to see you! Pull that chair close, sweetie. I ordered up a spare cup for you, and there's oceans of coffee."

The instant she handed him the cup her mood changed. Her mouth trembled. "Brownie, I have to talk to you. There's nobody else."

"Just George and Ida."

"Their minds are made up. No matter what I said, they'd still be convinced I'm being an idiot. I guess there is room for doubt. I don't know. Brownie, I trust you. I want you to tell me honestly if I'm being a fool."

39

"Or do you want me to confirm something you've already decided?"

"Maybe you know too much about me, too. But you will listen? You will tell me what you *really* think?"

"You know I will."

"I'm so lucky they put you on this script thing. I suppose because we're friends, they did that. Terrible coffee, isn't it? Brownie, I've got to tell you all about last night. From the beginning."

Her mind, conditioned by all the memorizing of parts and lyrics over the years, rebuilt the conversations for him. And her actress talent duplicated the way they were said.

Tom had driven her to the Wimpole Street address, a small stone building with a look of dignity. There were lights on the second floor. She had told Tom not to wait. He had seemed a little upset. She told him she would take a taxi.

"The lights came on and a Miss Plimpton answered the bell. A nurse-secretary sort of person. Quite pretty. Young and sort of pale and quite bosomy and veddy veddy correct. She said that Mr. Donne was expecting me. That was something I didn't know. When you're a surgeon, you're Mister instead of Doctor. She led me back through a foyer and a reception hall and up a curvy staircase. I got part way up and I saw David up there, standing by the railing in the shadows. It's almost fourteen years, Brownie. A long time. It has to be awkward, I suppose. And I guess it was more awkward because I was forcing myself upon him. He was a handsome young man, Brownie. And now he is a very distinguished-looking man. His features are stronger. He looks fit. Going gray at the temples and over the ears. And, of course, that damned British control. I think they take their men out someplace at age thirty and pump their faces full of cement."

She had looked up at him and said, "David . . . ?"

"How are you, Jenny?"

"Is this terribly inconvenient?"

"I don't think so. Come on up."

She went up and David took her coat and handed it to Miss Plimpton who carried it along the upper corridor and into the consulting room. Behind David Jenny saw a door partially open and beyond it a fire in a hearth, comfortable chairs. Jenny moved toward it and said, "Through here?"

David had effortlessly politely blocked her way. "That's for social calls. You did want to see me professionally, did you now?"

"Yes, doctor. A business call."

"Then we go this way, please." He led the way to the consulting room, where Miss Plimpton stood by the examination chair, under the cold bright medical lighting. He led Jenny over to his desk, seated her, took out a card. "Now if you will tell me what is wrong." He looked poised, sympathetic and absolutely neutral.

"I suppose you were surprised to hear from me."

"A little," he said, and made a notation on the card. "You sang this evening. Charity concert, wasn't it? How did it go?"

"Ghastly."

"Of course. That means you were good."

"No. It's true. My throat was raw. I couldn't produce anything. I couldn't swallow." She glanced at Miss Plimpton. "Am I keeping your nurse?"

"No. She works here."

"But this is really awfully late for her, isn't it?"

"Please tell me the rest of your symptoms. It's rather late for all of us, I suspect."

"I . . . I suddenly felt scared I was losing my voice, David."

"When did that fear start?"

"When? Oh . . . since I got to England. And don't tell me it's the climate. I thrive on this kind of climate."

"This is something which has happened previously?"

"Years ago."

"In Europe?"

"In New York. And my voice did go. And a young English doctor who just happened to be studying there at the time cured me."

David stopped writing and studied her for a long expressionless moment. "I believe we should have a look. Would you come this way, please?"

She sat in the examination chair. He put on the reflector mirror and picked up the speculum. "How are your sinuses?"

"I guess you'll have to tell me."

He tilted her head back gently, dilated her nostrils in turn with the instrument, examined her. "Any colds recently? Hoarseness?"

"No."

"You used to have colds frequently as I recall."

"I take vitamins."

He handed the speculum to Miss Plimpton and she gave him a tongue depressor.

"Open your mouth widely, please."

"You've gotten gray, David."

"I'm an old man. Open your mouth." He inspected her throat, made her say ah. "Now," he said, "we shall have a look at the larynx." Miss Plimpton had warmed the laryngeal mirror over a spirit lamp and tested it on her wrist before handing it to David. "You remember the proced . . ."

"I can remember it without liking it. Stick out my tongue, concentrate on breathing quietly in and out through my mouth, and you hold my tongue with that nasty piece of gauze. Yes indeed, I remember. I shall relax, David dear, and think of something pleasant."

When he had finished and put the mirror aside, she said, "Would you like to know what I was thinking about?"

He walked around behind her and began gently fingering the glands and muscles of her neck and throat. "Tell me if you feel any pain."

"I was thinking of Atlantic City. Do you ever think of Atlantic City? Would you call it a pleasant thought, David?"

"Perhaps. Does this give you any pain?"

"N-No."

"Swallow, please. Thank you." He walked around in front of her.

"Am I going to lose my voice?"

"What do you think, Jenny?"

"There's nothing wrong with me?"

He took off the reflector and handed it to Miss Plimpton. He went to the desk. Jenny followed him. He took out a prescription form.

"Your throat is a bit red, the membranes slightly roughened. After all, you have been singing. And you smoke too much. When do you open your regular stint here?"

"In five days."

"I shall give you something to ease that minor irritation, Jenny. And if you have five days, I strongly urge you to take off three of them. Rest, sleep, relaxation."

"Where can I buy that?"

"And I would like to have you gargle with this morning and evening."

She sauntered over to the sliding doors which she suspected must open into the fireplace room she had seen before. "Couldn't you prescribe an immediate drink?"

He looked up quickly and smiled, stood up and put the prescription slip in his jacket pocket. "You were determined to go in there, weren't you? Very well." He slid the door open. "Come along, if you must."

They went into the small living room. David went to the bar cabinet. Jenny went to look into the mirror over the fireplace mantel to touch her hair, freshen her lipstick.

"Still Scotch, I suppose?"

"With a little water, please." Glancing at him in the mirror she saw him move to screen with his body the quick motion with which he turned a picture face down. He brought her drink to her and she turned and accepted it, smiling.

"No ice, I'm afraid. Please be comfortable, Jenny." He indicated a chair. He went to the sliding doors and closed them as Jenny sat.

"You have changed, David."

"Wouldn't it be rather alarming if I hadn't?" he said and came smiling toward her and took the chair opposite hers. He lifted his drink. "Salud!"

"David, you've become so . . . so guarded. No. That's not quite the right word. Careful?"

She thought he looked slightly dismayed. "Have I? Perhaps. Care comes, I imagine. It comes. Possibly the more we acquire in this world the more careful we become . . . trying to hold to it."

"I heard about Janet's death. I do have her name right?"

"Janet, yes. I read about your marriage."

"Which one? Not that it makes any difference. Neither of them were worth . . . the time it took to read about them. I should have married you. It would have worked, you know. It really would have worked."

He looked at her somberly and shook his head. "You're wrong, Jenny."

"You seem so sure of that, don't you?"

"It is better as it is."

She stood up quickly and began to wander restlessly around the room, agitated but trying to control herself. "Very cozy here, David. Nice and sort of worn and calm and safe. Who keeps it up for you?" He did not answer. She picked up a small recorder from a table, replaced it, turned and smiled at him, "Don't tell me you've given up your study of the harmonica!"

"Completely. Too many complaints. Do you still knit?"

"Rarely." They looked at each other, both smiling, caught in old memories. She said with a trace of wistfulness, "We must have had fun. I remember it that way, at least. Did we have fun, really? Please tell me."

"Yes."

"See? I can twist your arm. Obviously, I've come here just to rake up old ashes. Looking for an ember, maybe."

"Why did you come, Jenny?"

"The truth? Maybe I just didn't want to be alone my first night in a strange city."

"You must have scores of friends in London, just as you have everywhere else. You wouldn't have been alone."

She looked in the mirror, then turned toward him with that special urgency of despair. "I've made such a mess of things, David. Maybe it's not my throat, but there's something. They say I have an audience in every city in the world. But I haven't a home anywhere. All my life I've . . . I've been throwing away everything that really matters." She shivered. "I'm so awfully tired, David. . . ." She tried to fight her way back toward casualness. "Who does your flowers? Miss Plimpton?"

David was watching her closely. "Why don't you sit down, Jenny."

She wandered over to the drink cabinet and looked at a picture of David in evening dress being presented to the Queen Mother.

"Some sort of a ceremony?"

"I was being given the OBE. One gets it for taking out precisely the right set of tonsils." She ran her finger along the rim of the picture that was face down, knowing he was watching her carefully. "May I fix a drink?" he asked.

"Thank you, no." She picked up the picture and turned it over and looked at it. A young boy smiled out at her. The face looked vital and sensitive, much as David might have looked as a boy, she thought. "Why did you hide this from me, David?"

"Hide it? My word, why should I hide it?"

"Oh, David. Really. I saw you turn it face down."

"Then I must have hidden it."

There was a gentle knock at the door and Miss Plimpton entered at once, bringing Jenny's coat. "Excuse me, Mr. Donne, but would you need me for anything further?"

"Nothing more, thank you. I'm sorry, Miss Plimpton. It's very late and I should have told you you could go. I'll see Miss Bowman out. How does tomorrow look?"

"The Clinic at 8:30 . . . the Williams girl . . . Mrs. Hurley at 11:45, with X-rays and Major Somerset at 12:15. And of course Miss Spicer in the afternoon."

"Thank you. Good night, Miss Plimpton."

"Good night, sir. Good night, Miss Bowman. May I say how much I enjoy your singing?"

"Thank you."

When the door clicked shut, Jenny put the boy's picture on the cabinet and looked at him, trying to find some trace of herself in him, possibly around his eyes. "Is he here, David?"

"No. He's at school. He boards."

"David. I want to see him."

"So now, at last, at long last, we come to the point, do we?"

"Please, David, I swear to you I didn't come here to ask that. I came to see you. I admit that. But now . . . I have to ask you . . . please let me see him."

"I'm sorry. You can't see him. It's that simple. You can't."

Her own flash of anger startled her. "Why the hell not? Is he invisible? Is he an idiot? Does he have the plague? Is the school on the back of the moon?"

"I'm sorry. It's impossible."

She controlled herself. "Impossible is a word I seldom hear, David," she said quietly.

"I'm sorry it has to come as such a surprise to you."

"I want to see him!"

"Can't you comprehend what I'm saying to you? It is *impossible*. That was the agreement. That was the way it was arranged. Surely you remember."

"Yes. I remember. But do you want to know something? I didn't know what that word 'never' meant. I didn't know how that word could ache. I guess I thought . . . hoped . . ." She walked to the chair that held her coat. "The only real and true thing I ever created in my life . . . and then I had to let all of them convince me I had to . . ." She trembled, suddenly close to tears, turned her face away from him and fought them down. "Does he like school?"

"He loves it, actually."

"Is he clever?"

"Average, I'd judge. Better at Mozart than math."

"Musical, you mean?"

"Rather odd if he weren't, don't you think?"

"Perhaps, but I loathed Mozart."

"Jenny, you can be proud of him. Be satisfied with that."

"Let me see him."

"No."

"Just once. Please."

"And then what?"

"Then nothing. I go."

After a thoughtful moment, David said, "Do believe me, Jenny, when I say I know what this must be costing you. And has cost you. I hoped, for your sake, there would be other children. If I thought it would make anything better for you, I would let you see him. But were you to see him now, it would merely make things that much more difficult . . . for you."

She started to put on her coat, listlessly. "I've barged in on you, kept you up, stayed too long. I'm sorry. I'd better go."

He helped her with her coat. "Have you a car waiting?"

"No. I was going to get a taxi. But I think I'd rather walk. And I'll let myself out. Don't bother. You've been very kind, David. Thank you."

She heard him close behind her as she went down the narrow curving staircase. As they reached the reception hall he said, "Jenny?" She turned quickly and expectantly. He held out the prescription slip. "Don't forget this."

She tucked it into her purse. "What will it cure?"

"Perhaps it will help a little."

She wanted to smile at him, and tried valiantly, but the tears clotted her lashes, spilled.

"It really would mean a great deal to you to see him, wouldn't it?"

"Yes," she whispered. "Oh, yes."

"And if I should permit this, against my own better judgment, and mark that phrase, Jenny . . . *permit* this . . . do you promise on your word of honor that you will be content with that one meeting, and never try to see him again?"

"I promise," she said.

There were tears in her eyes again as she looked at Jason Brown. "You see, I really didn't know I was going to ask that of him, Brownie. Maybe I did know, but I hadn't admitted it to myself. I told myself I was going just to see him. He's a part of my life, maybe the biggest part. I bore his child. Maybe I love him."

"When does this happen?"

"He's stopping by for me early this afternoon. He rearranged his schedule. The school isn't too far, really. Oh,

Brownie, I'm so scared and excited! Lift this tray away, will you please?"

He took it away and put it on the floor near the closed door. She swung her legs out of bed, scuffed her feet into her slippers, paced and smoked, pausing at the mirrors for the quick touch at her hair, the absent-minded examination of her face. She whirled and stared at him, her eyes very wide, "Tell me I'm insane."

"What was he like, really?"

"There was a lot of tension. Undercurrents. Little memories of things past running through his mind as well as mine. And the fraudulent professional visit, with the Plimpton person standing there. But you see, don't you, that he could have absolutely refused to see me at all? Even if he believed it was an emergency, he could have had another doctor there to see me. That's what I kept remembering, that with all his reserve, and patronizing me as if I was some sort of idiot child, he still had curiosity about me. And it must have unsettled him, knowing I was coming. Otherwise, he would have hidden Matthew's picture away before I got there. Brownie, darling, I deal with people under stress all the time, and they can't hide all the signs. He couldn't. Matthew. Isn't that a nifty name? Matthew Donne. But they call him Matt. I wouldn't permit that. What do you wear to go visit your boy at school? Look at me! Slow death. I couldn't sleep, not for a minute. I don't know why we couldn't send out for good coffee in the morning, or see if Lois could make it here, maybe. Ida makes horrible coffee. And you remember mine."

"Essence of battery acid."

"Brownie, you sit there and you smile, and you are a dear gangling rumply old pet, but you're not *saying* anything. How is your little girl?"

"Frightening. She's a blonde, like Joyce. All female wiles and devices."

"Brownie, bless you, do you remember an utterly impossible day in Mexico City? What a slob I was? The tears and the drinks, and running away from you and nearly getting run down by a taxi?"

"I remember."

"That was Matthew's sixth birthday. And those days haven't gotten any better for me. Worse, if anything. Every year I tell myself it's just another day, after all. Brownie, what if the world took your little girl away and you could never see her again or write to her or know anything about her. How would her birthdays be for you?"

"Wretched."

"Brownie, I'm right! Tell me I'm right!" She came and put her hands on his shoulders and looked into his eyes, bending down toward him.

"Jenny, if you were sure you're right, you wouldn't be asking me."

She backed away. "You are too plain damned smart about me. How did you get so smart about me?"

"By loving you."

"My God, you're slippery as an eel. When I try to get mad at you, you touch my heart. All right. I loved you too. We were good for each other, weren't we? In all the hideous confusion of my life, Brownie, you were . . . you were a little island of content, and I cherish the memories. Be good for me now. *Help* me!"

"No matter what I say, you are going to go see the boy. And it is going to shred you, Jenny. It's going to stomp your heart raw. And then you are going to have to turn your back on him and walk away. And that act is going to take all the guts and pride and spirit you have. It's a test of strength."

She walked slowly to the bed and sat and stared at him. "Am I strong enough?"

"You have to be. You have no other choice, Jenny."

"It was a mistake to come to England?"

"Of course."

She nodded. Her smile was wan. "But, you see, I had no other choice there, either. Do you know what I mean?"

"I think so."

"I guess you better go now. Thank you, Brownie. I guess I am going to cry for a little while now, and then get dressed."

He stopped by the door and said, "Did you tell George where you're going?"

"Not even Ida."

"I better let them know, don't you think?"

"Anything you say. Just be sure to tell George not to try to set up anything for me today."

He opened the door, picked up the tray and carried it out. When he looked back, closing the door, he saw that she had turned to lie face down across the bed. He saw the yellow robe and her dark hair and thought she looked small. And lost, somehow.

Ida was sitting by the windows taking stitches in the bodice of a glittering gown. She looked up, eyebrows raised in query.

"The doctor is driving her out to see the boy at school today."

"The good Lord preserve us all," she said.

He put the tray on a table near the corridor door. "Ida, how was it for her, when they were making her give up the baby?"

She looked startled and then she looked through him into the past. "It was a savage thing," she said softly. "The money machine was breaking down and they had to fix it or the money would stop. So . . . they fixed it. Sometimes I wonder . . ."

"Wonder what?"

She sighed. "If we're any better. George and I. All of us. Saying we love her. All this loyalty. But maybe it's the life we want. The glamor machine? And we get our part of it and get used to it, then tell ourselves we're thinking of her good. I don't know. Eighteen years now. It's a poor time to have doubts."

"It depends on what she really wants, Ida."

"Maybe, just for the hell of it, she wants to be a woman. George was in. You better tell him what's going on. He's right across the hall, and I think he's still in there."

Jason Brown crossed the corridor and knocked on George's door. In a moment it opened, Lois Marney looked out at him and opened the door the rest of the way. She smiled openly yet shyly, then greeted him and turned quickly away. She wore a gray-green shirtwaist blouse with long sleeves, a pleated skirt in a darker shade of green. George was on the phone saying, ". . . please don't try to tell me that, Harkness. I am not interested in what a triumph of modern color press stuff you got over there. Believe me, I am interested in Jenny Bowman because I am paid to be interested in her, and the proof you sent me, I swear to you my first thought was you got mixed up and sent me a picture of Apple Annie. If it was my job to scare people away, I would say yes, we should use it. I wouldn't dare show it to her. I'm telling you, you've got to make a new plate. I'm sorry, but that's the way it is. And I will have a good attitude. If it looks even a little like Jenny Bowman, we'll approve it, okay?" As he listened, he looked over at Jason and winked. Then he said, "By Thursday. Fine. What's that? Four tickets? Harkness, I could not get my own mother four for the Friday opening, but I can put a reserve on four for Saturday, if you don't mind they aren't real choice. They'll be at the box office in your name. Right. Thanks a lot."

He hung up and said, "Lois, put down . . ."

"I've got it."

George ran fingers through thinning hair and stared at Jason. "Don't tell me. Let me guess. She and the doctor are flying to Cannes for a second honeymoon and we scratch the London engagement."

"He's picking her up early this afternoon and driving her out to the school where the boy is."

George sat on the bed. "Now isn't that just dandy! Picking her up here. And the press people hanging around the lobby, all ready to follow them out there. Maybe they can get some nice pictures of the three of them. Star reunited with give-away baby. The indiscretion kid. Lois, you better go work up that stuff while I figure out how to smuggle her out of here."

Lois Marney stood up and picked up her purse and black cardigan and left.

"I make it sound hard," George said, "but it's no problem. I'm just getting a little gun shy. And my gut is acting up. It's like an old bullet wound. It anticipates trouble. Sorry I had to fold so quick last night."

"You left me in good hands, George."

"Lois is a good kid. Without her taking care, this whole thing would fall apart. Of course, maybe it will anyway."

"And you say she's been with you over two and a half years?"

George gave him a quick shrewd look. "Aha! The merchandise intrigues. You wouldn't be trying to pump me, old buddy. My God, your face is turning red, Jase! I would have had to see it to believe it. I am sorry, pal, but you better just cross it off your list."

"She has other plans?"

"Just say she has no plans at all, and nobody can sell her any plans. It all looks very delicious indeed. But all you get to do is look. I think she took too much of a bruise in that marriage. Maybe it knotted her all up too much. But you know this cruddy industry, Jase. Some experts have zeroed in on her and struck out swinging, much to their astonishment. We did a television special with Kirby King last year. He decided he wanted it, and he went after it, and I'd guess he hasn't missed once since he was sixteen years old. He tried every approach he'd ever used or ever heard of, and I think he made up some new ones nobody had ever heard of before. Nothing worked, and he was getting pretty sullen about it, and finally he decided he would just plan grab her, figuring maybe that after she finished jumping and yelping he could gentle her down. But she didn't jump and she didn't yelp. She just went limp, and as soon as she had the chance, she brought the knee up. Kirb lost all interest in her forever. He hobbled around like a little old man for days and days. So you'll have to figure out something else if you want to sweeten this little junket. It shouldn't be hard, pal. The town is loaded."

"So is the Coast, George. And always has been. And I went that route for a while, and eventually it turns into the dreariest thing in the world."

"Jason, we are getting old."

He smiled at George. "And I find it restful. When you get to the point where you have to stop proving things. So old, in fact, that I would far prefer an unsuccessful pursuit of your Lois Marney to a custom bed teeming with nubile little English lassies."

"You turn a nice phrase, Jason. A nice phrase. So be our guest. Lois is fun to talk to and fun to be with, and she won't let you get in the way of the work she has to do. I shall even tell her you are a very nice guy. But it won't do you a bit of good. Now get out of here because I have to get on the phone and do more battles."

As Jason Brown reached the door, George said, "Is that Jamison script as good as it seemed to me when I read it?"

"George, it is so good that to force any other writer to read it is cruel and unusual punishment."

"It would be the best thing she ever did in her life?"

"Beyond the shadow of a doubt."

"Maybe she knows that, Jase. Maybe she wants it. Maybe that's the best hope we have."

five

FOR JASON BROWN it was a strange, aimless, restless day,
filled with the tension of waiting. He envied George Kogan
and Lois Marney all the detail work that kept them busy.
Jenny, after four complete and frantic changes, had set off
in a dark suit, cloth coat trimmed and lined with fur, a
little mink hat and a big mink muff. George, properly wary
of the British press, had intercepted the doctor at the desk,
and then smuggled Jenny out a service entrance. He reported
that the doctor looked a little younger than he had expected,
quite a handsome guy, maybe a little too handsome. And
Jenny had been pale as chalk, her hands shaking. They had
taken off in the doctor's Humber, the doctor driving.

For George and Lois, the biggest problem was how to re-
schedule, without ruffling too many feelings, the press, magazine, radio and television interviews which had been set up
for Jenny and approved by her—how to sense which ones
could be safely canceled, and which ones had to be fitted
into the scheduling of the following days prior to her opening. It required a combination of guile, judgment, flattery
and good sense. And the throat problem, imaginary as it
was, came in handy, and might eventually be of tactical
use in explaining any association with Doctor Donne.

Jason heard George say, with the same impeccable sincerity, a dozen times, "She really gave last night, sweetheart.
She belted more than she was supposed to. So, I swear, she's
taking it easy today. We can't take any chances. You understand that. She wants to talk to you particularly. She's very
very upset about having to change things around a little,
and she hopes you won't be mad at her."

In the late afternoon, after a walk in the clearing weather,
and after writing a letter to Bonny and buying a present
for her and having it sent airmail, Jason wandered back to
the Park Lane. George was in Lois's room, stretched out on
the chaise, drink in hand. Lois was typing up the revised
schedule for the balance of the week. She gave Jason a quick

smile and turned back to her typewriter. At George's invitation, Jason fixed himself a drink.

"Now what we do," George said, "we hope that she doesn't have something all worked up for tomorrow too."

"Hush," Lois said without interrupting her typing speed.

"Most of the time," George said thoughtfully, "Jenny is real good about these things. But when she goofs . . ."

"Hush," Lois said again.

"That's the weird thing about this business," George said. "You've seen it enough times, Jase. No temperament at all usually means no talent either, right? And too much temperament usually means no talent, too. But when you get as big as Jenny is, suppose like three percent of the time you fling your weight around. What happens, the press people make it sound like ninety percent. How many times in her life has she walked out of a commitment? Seven? Eight? Maybe ten even? And how many times has she gone on, how many hundreds and hundreds of times, even when everything was falling down on her head?"

"Nothing like what could fall down this time," Jason said. "Stop reminding me."

Jason moved over toward the typing table and looked over Lois Marney's shoulder. It was his intention to look at the new schedule. But he found himself looking at the nape of Lois's neck. She sat so erect the small of her back was concave. It was a strong-looking neck. The skin was very smooth. There were small curling tendrils of blonde hair. He pretended to be looking at the schedule and he looked at her neck. Somehow the neck of this mature woman made him think of pussy willows. He knew it was an awkward simile, but he happened to be stuck with it. He wanted to press his mouth to the nape of that neck, wanted so badly that it dizzied him for a moment. He took a deep breath of her fragrance and moved away, swallowing against the dryness in his mouth.

She pulled the sheets out of the machine, separated the carbons deftly. She got up and took the original over to George. Again Jason Brown was aware of the special way she moved. She was a tall woman with a strong rounded body, and though her hands were very quick and deft, she moved with constraint, like a fine taut mare too accustomed to the hobble.

George said, "If everything else goes fine, it is still going to be a good trick getting her on the beam by ten in the morning."

"Predawn, practically," Lois said.

"Can your slave labor take a break?" Jason asked George. They both stared at him. "There's a park and the weather has cleared, and some daylight left."

"I've got some things I could . . ."

"Go take a walk, sweetie," George said. "I'm spoiling you. I gave you a twelve-minute lunch break even." He got up, winked at Lois and left the room.

She frowned at Jason. "Really, I ought to . . ."

"You ought to see a little bit of London."

She smiled and shrugged. "See you in the lobby in five minutes, Jason."

She appeared within the allotted time, in lower heels, with a gray tweed cape over her green suit, hair freshly brushed and gleaming, lipstick freshened.

He walked her to the nearest pedestrian entrance to Hyde Park. The air was clear and cool in the watery sunlight of late afternoon. Traffic roar faded behind them as he lengthened his stride, glad of the way she swung along with him.

"All this is technically royal property," he told her. "Originally a private hunting preserve for old Henry the Eighth. They took out a lot of old trees along here recently. Lot of fuss about it. Angry letters to the *Times*. A lot of trees came out along that stretch there. Rotten Row it's called."

"What a horrible name for such a pretty place!"

"It's a corruption of Route du Roi, meaning King's Way."

"You're practically a professional guide, Jason," she said with a sidelong look of amusement and respect.

"Hardly. I've got one of those minds that useless pieces of information stick to. And this is my fourth trip to London."

"My first. The first time I've ever even been out of the United States."

As they walked he told her about the Serpentine, and John Rennie's bridge, and the Ring, and the Tea House and the Powder Magazine, and the Kinsington Gardens wall. They sat on a bench. She was flushed with the exercise and the coolness of the air.

"Thanks for prying me loose, Jason. It's good to . . . get away from there."

"I wanted to be with you," he said bluntly.

She gave him a wary glance and looked away. "Look at the women in those lovely robes, Jason."

"Saris."

"When was the first time you were in London?"

"A long time ago."

She made a face at him. "You're truly ancient, aren't you?"

"Compared to then, yes. I was a fearless warrior, aged nineteen. Company clerk in an infantry company because I knew how to type. Got here four months before D-Day. Intensive training. The company landed at Omaha Beach, but Fearless Warrior was in a hospital thirty miles from London. I was looking at the sky and walked into a ditch and broke my leg. And while I was in the hospital I caught the measles."

She laughed. "Poor Jason. I was thirteen on D-Day. And I had a lot of excitement too. I stole a negative of my big sister in a bathing suit and had scads of copies made and sent them to soldiers and sailors and marines, with letters pledging undying love and devotion. I loved them all, really and truly. I was safe while they were all overseas, but some of them got leave and came looking for me. I was as tall as I am now, and weighed about ninety-eight pounds including my braces. And I had a stammer and a horrible complexion. I was a disappointment to them. After I confessed, I had to come straight home from school for a month. No allowance. No movies. And even my little red radio was impounded."

"I wanted to be with you," he said again.

She flushed and said, "The thing that really has George edgy is the idea of what it will do to the Jenny Bowman image if this thing about the boy comes out. You see, so much of the image depends on warmth, Jason. And she is such a warm woman. But even I had to have it explained to me, how such a thing could be, giving away a child like that. He thinks it will make the public believe the whole business of the warmth is an act, always has been an act, that she is really a cold and selfish woman. He doesn't see how it could ever be presented in such a way her public will forgive her."

"It must not be found out."

"But she's being reckless. Coming here was reckless. Going to see the boy is very dangerous."

"The doctor may have some sense."

"But he took her to see the boy. Is that sensible? What *good* will it do?"

He reached and took her hand. She made one effort to pull free, and then let her hand remain passive in his. "Lois, I wanted to be with you."

She looked out across the grassy park. "You're with me," she said in a toneless voice.

"Last night I . . ."

"Last night I was tired and lonely and vulnerable, Jason."

"What I want to say, I wasn't making a pass. Not in that sense of making a pass."

She pulled her hand away. "That's nice to know. That's dandy. Three separate times today George has managed to let me know what a darling man you are. I think that's a terribly sweet gesture on his part, don't you?"

"Lois, I just want to . . ."

"Be my friend? Be my dear friend?" She stared at him, gray eyes frigid. "All righty. Be my friend then. Walk me around and be a guide book and share my little secretarial problems, but kindly leave it right there. Okay?"

"What are you scared of?"

Her lip curled in a rather unpleasant way. "Isn't that sort of a cheap and obvious question, Jason? That could lead us into that dialogue you talked about last night. Oh me oh my, I'm scared of life, scared of love, scared of myself. And here you are, to cure all my silly fears. Nuts, Jason. Nothing in this world scares me."

"Loneliness?"

Her smile was thin. "We can't have everything, can we? Maybe I get a little lonely on rainy nights. But it just doesn't rain that often. I need no help, my friend. No pillar of strength, thank you so much. You fell in love with Jenny when she was shattered. And your wife was . . . an inadequate. I'm sane and sound and whole and dandy, Jason. I'll provide my own strength, when needed, thanks."

He smiled at her. "You can lick any woman in the house."

"Bring 'em on!" she said, blushing.

"We'll take you to the Marble Arch on Sunday, Lois, and you can stand on a box and explain to the multitude why you don't need anyone or anything."

"Did I sound like that?"

"A little bit."

"I'm sorry. It . . . it's sort of a reflex, I guess. These past two years working for George. In this business a girl who won't play becomes sort of a minor legend. A real challenge or something. So I come out swinging. A little too hard, maybe."

"You win on a TKO in the first round, Miss Marney. I am a tiresome old party with a nervous stomach, a four-year-old daughter, a few screen credits, too few friends, too many acquaintances, a long history of emotional ineptitude and romantic bungling, no reserve for contingencies, and a present assignment I don't like and couldn't avoid. But I like you, Miss Marney. You take wild swings without good reason, but I like the way you walk and the way you look, and I think I like the way your mind works. If I make any passes at all, they'll be that tentative kind you can block with one elbow. If we can just think of them as unavoidable male reflexes, a sop to my pride and a concession to your attractiveness, we can ignore them and be pretty good friends."

She frowned at him. "You're strange," she said. "You are either a very honest man or you are a terrible sneak."

"Lois, my dear, were I a sneak, I would have been one hell of a lot more successful in the industry."

She laughed abruptly. "Okay, Jason. When I was going to sleep last night I decided to chill you good. And ignore you henceforth. But we will be friends."

They shook hands and got up. The sun was gone, the shadows heavy. They walked slowly back toward the distant lights of the traffic of Park Lane and Piccadilly. After several minutes of silence, Lois said, "You didn't hurt her, did you?"

"Jenny? No."

"Because we're friends now, I can ask you a question like that without you taking it wrong, can't I?"

"Of course."

"She can be terribly difficult."

"She was too beaten down to be difficult seven years ago. I was therapy. I didn't know it at the time, of course. No more than she did. We thought it was forever. It was a very quiet thing with us, and intense. But now I can see other reasons why it wouldn't have worked."

"Like?"

"Her mind works in specifics. Specific emotions, wants, needs. Incident and anecdote. It's a very mercurial mind. But any abstract conjecture, any kind of subjective thought makes her itchy and restless. And I'm always thinking of things which have no utility at all. Like a moment ago wondering why these British gentlemen furl their umbrellas so tightly, and why they refold their newspapers so carefully they look unread."

"Why do they?"

"Well, for a guess, the effect of the population density

over such a long period, a necessity for neatness, for taking up a minimum of space, a kind of tidiness that relates to all the other more necessary kinds. See what I mean? You were instantly curious. Jenny couldn't care less. So maybe we both have trivial minds."

She chuckled. He asked her why she laughed. "I caught that one on my elbow," she said.

"Was it a pass?"

"Of course."

"Inadvertent, though."

She looked at him, her face solemn in the dusk, owlish. "Oh, but those are the worst kind."

When they walked into the lobby, a voice behind Jason said, "They'll give almost anybody a passport these days."

Jason turned and looked down into the bland and smiling face of Sam Dean. "We're both astonished," Jason said woodenly.

Sam bowed toward Lois. "Our startled chum has forgotten his manners, my dear. I am Sam Dean."

"Miss Marney," Jason said. "Miss Marney is . . ."

"Yes indeed," Sam said. "I know. Kirby King mentioned you with a certain amount of heat and emphasis, my dear. In his circle you are known as the stone butterfly. May I say that I admire his taste and deplore his tactics."

Lois looked nervous. "Mr. Dean, if we'd known you were in London, we would certainly have set up . . ."

"All arranged, my dear. I had a lovely drink with lovely George. I just got in today. From Athens. Incredible sunlight there. Skit and Marielana and Hobey are there, working on that ghastly television thing. Is Jenny booked into Athens? No? Too bad. George should arrange it, really. Why don't you run along, my dear, while I have a nice chat with my old chum, Jason."

She looked at Jason nervously. He nodded and she walked toward the elevators.

Sam Dean watched her, approvingly, and said, "Everyone seems so jumpy around here, Jason."

"You make people jumpy, Sam. Everybody gets jumpy in the presence of an assassin."

Sam Dean looked at him, momentarily startled, and then lifted his chin higher and laughed. It was a small thin squealing laugh. "You amuse me, dear boy. You know why you can afford to be impertinent? You're too small a target. I'd look ridiculous, aiming a broadside at Jason Brown. People would wonder who the hell I was talking about. Let's find a drink in this tomb."

Jason followed Sam Dean into the lounge. Dean was a small frail man. His shoulders were thick and broad, and he carried them high and slightly hunched. He had almost no neck at all, and carried his narrow head tilted in a way that gave him the look of a hunchback, though he was not deformed. In New York, Palm Springs, Vegas, London, Miami, Acapulco, he was always dressed exactly the same way, black suits, beautifully tailored, black knit ties, highly polished black shoes, black socks, gold accessories, fresh white gleaming shirt and handkerchief. The rims of his thick lenses were gold. His hair was dark, his face pale and narrow, his eyes dark. He was always freshly barbered, manicured, immaculate. The only touch of color was the heavy red sensuous mouth.

No one knew exactly where he came from. They said he started out as a movie reviewer on a Philadelphia paper. No one knew how old he was. His show business gossip column—"The Dean's List"—was syndicated in over two hundred papers. It was fed and fattened by nervous press agents who complied with Sam Dean's six-to-one ratio. If you fed him six useable extraneous items, then he would accept one which plugged a client. He seldom had to write anything for the column. He had a New York office where a small staff put it together. Once in a while Sam Dean would write the lead paragraphs for the column. His touch was unmistakable. What he wrote would sound very warm and tolerant and slightly heartbroken that a public figure should be betraying the trust of an adoring public by some sort of private vice or recklessness. The general tenor was an admonition to shape up, mend your ways, and all will be forgiven. The usual result was so much panic on the part of the purse-string people that Sam Dean's target slid quickly into obscurity.

He was known in the entertainment world as The Hangman.

It was also generally known in the industry that Sam Dean owned the controlling interest in Century Celebrities, Inc. This was a small public relations firm which seemed to do a minimum of public relations work. But it had a long client list. People who became a little too vulnerable seemed to learn that if they contracted with Century Celebrities at, say, two hundred a week, any mention of them which appeared in

"The Dean's List" would be favorable. And when MCA was forced to drop its agency business, a new firm called Century Representation, Inc. appeared, and many of the people who had contracted with the first firm began to be represented by the second. Also there were producers in cinema, television and the legitimate theater who always seemed quite eager to give Sam Dean a little piece of the action when something looked good.

Sam Dean had become a very rich man. Feared with a cold fear—hated with a murderous intensity. But everyone was agreed on one aspect of his success. He never invented the unpleasantness he exposed. He checked facts. He had never lost a major suit. The column was larded with minor inaccuracies, but when he really dropped the boom, he had a file to back it up.

With a glass of cream sherry in his hand, Sam Dean smiled at Jason Brown and said, "I thought you had disappeared entirely and forever, dear boy, after your fleeting moments of notoriety. How long ago was it? Seven years. Don't tell me you and Jenny have gotten hooked on nostalgia."

"What's the matter, Sam? You picked the time when she was really down, and then you tried to kick her to death. Does it bother you that she came back?"

Sam Dean looked amused. "You don't understand these things, Jason. She was a public institution at the time. She had a responsibility to the public. That was a very messy divorce, you know. And she should have been spending her time bolstering a good public image instead of running off to Mexico with you."

"So it was your duty to expose the whole filthy situation?"

"I am—in a certain sense—a watchdog, Jason." He sipped the sherry, smacked his red lips and said, "Be grateful. I gave you national coverage."

Jason stared at him in a brooding way. "You know, I don't mind that so much. I can almost understand it. But I can't ever forgive or forget that little notice you gave me when I married Joyce, or the little sour thing you put in there when Joyce was killed."

"You sound as if I had some personal interest. Don't be absurd, dear boy. When you became intimate with Jenny, you became newsworthy. And my public likes to know what happens to the ex-friends of the stars. What do you expect when you marry an alcoholic? Immunity? A conspiracy of silence?"

"Jenny is going to be delighted to see you."

He finished the sherry, gestured for another. "Don't be naive, Jason. Really! I've talked to Jenny many times since you and she broke up. She's not a fool. I'm one of the facts of life of her profession, like agents and taxes. We get along quite well. She has a professional attitude. You are an incurable amateur. But what in the world are you doing here?"

Jason knew he did not dare hesitate too long. "I'm working on the script of her next moving picture. I came over to check a few things with her."

"Didn't I read she was going to do a Jamison thing?"

"That's what this script is. And damned good, too."

Sam Dean frowned. "Then where could you possibly fit into the picture? Don't answer that question. Let me see. As far as I know, she's still fond of you. Suppose she was balking at doing the picture. Or she doesn't care for the choice of director or leading man. She and Wegler don't get along. Jamison is a spook. This is very interesting. You and George Kogan were friendly, as I remember. Yes, if the lady was dragging her heels, Wegler might well send you over to smooth things out a little. Shooting would start after this tour, I suppose."

"Yes."

"Tell me, dear boy, just what trouble is Sid Wegler having with our Jenny?"

"I haven't heard of any."

"But there must be some sort of trouble. I'm not a fool. Dear George was too effusive. He never gets such a violent attack of the jollies unless he's trying to smoke-screen something. And that Marney woman turned pallid and shaky when she heard my name. And you have been glowering at me in a very uneasy way."

"I glower because I don't like you worth a damn, Sam."

"If I went around needing love, that could bother me. I think you should . . ." He jumped up quite spryly and gestured and smiled and snapped his fingers. The girl in the doorway saw him and came over to the table. Sam introduced them, telling the girl Jason was a famous author. Her name was Lydia Torres. She was very tall and very ripely built and very young. Sam Dean fussed over her, holding her chair, adjusting her wrap, ordering her a drink. She had blank blue eyes, a slack mouth and a dull bovine manner. According to rumor, Sam Dean had an endless source of supply of these, all of them equivalently young, big, healthy and slow-witted, evidently interchangeable. His quota seemed to be three or four of them a year. As soon as one disappeared, the next one appeared. And they all seemed to spend their time sitting at tables in night clubs with Sam Dean, sitting nested in fur, their shoulders bare, their hair intricately coifed, sipping their drinks and staring into the distance with a look of mild, patient boredom.

As soon as she was settled, Sam ignored her. He smiled at Jason. "Obviously you aren't going to tell me a thing. We were flying back Thursday, but I think now we shall stay until we find out what our Jenny is doing to make everyone so edgy."

"Everybody is edgy before an opening, Sam."

He smiled more broadly, like a fox reaching to nip the end off an egg. "If you should see darling Jenny before I do, Jason, tell her that Sam Dean hopes she is being a good girl. Tell her he sincerely hopes it, because it always hurts him to have to discipline one of the truly big names of the entertainment world. So nice to chat with you again after such a long, long time."

It was an effortless dismissal. When Jason looked back at them from the arched doorway he saw the two of them sitting there like wax figures, glossy, inert, staring into their separate segments of distance.

Lois, George and Ida Mulligan were in the sitting room of Jenny's suite. When George let him in, Jason said, "Is Jenny back?"

"Not yet. What did that little viper say?"

They were all looking intently at him. Jason sat down. Lois brought him a drink. He repeated all of the conversation that he could remember. George paced back and forth, snapping his fingers, cracking his knuckles.

When Jason had finished, George said, "This is just great! This is all we need. He's been gunning for her for years. He's written her off at least five times."

"Seven," Ida said. "She keeps track."

"I guess I don't understand," Lois said. "I know he writes terrible things about people. But how can he find out . . . about . . ."

George said irritably, "He keeps looking. When he thinks there's something worth looking for, he doesn't give up. He buys people. He gives them coarse pieces of money and they sign statements. He hires people to watch people. He hires people to bug phones and rooms, and steal letters and diaries. We've got to give him something that will steer him away from this situation."

"Like what?" Jason asked.

George stared at the ceiling for a moment. "Something about this movie?"

"That she doesn't want to do it? Is that strong enough?"

"He's a little bit creepy, isn't he?" Lois said.

George stared at her and gave a harsh and mirthless laugh. He began pacing again. "And where in the hell is our star?"

six

Jason Brown had seen joy. He had seen Jenny Bowman when she was happy. He had seen a great many volatile and excited people registering exuberant pleasure, but he had never seen anything quite like the Jenny Bowman who came into the suite at twenty minutes to midnight. She was glowing, spinning, laughing and crying, in a transport of joy. She wanted to share it all. She hugged and kissed them all, George, Lois, Jason, Ida, twice around, saying, "He's *adorable*! He's a *miracle*! He's a *charmer*! My son! Isn't that a wild thing to say? My son! I couldn't ever really say it out loud before. Mathew, my *son*."

"What happened to your shoes?" Ida demanded.

"Mud. Lovely gummy gooey mud from the playing fields of Canterbury School. They made him a fly half, you see, because Gregson broke his leg playing Eastbourne. And Matthew is really terribly fast. My very first sight of him was in this Rugger scrum—that even *sounds* muddy, doesn't it?—a great writhing mass of muddy little boys, and this little sodden *thing* came scooting out and the ball was kicked and he grabbed it and ran and David pointed him out and then all the rest of them came swarming down and piled onto him and I thought they would kill him and . . ."

"Whoa, girl," George said. "Slow down, girl."

She spun and dropped into a chair and beamed at them all and said, "I haven't been this happy in . . . in thirteen years, people."

"What kept you?"

"We stayed over for the end of term play. Matthew insisted. I feel so *good*, George."

"I don't want to be the one to fling a fly in the ointment, Jenny, but Sam Dean is registered here."

Her smile faded. She looked very alert and intent for a moment, her head tilted to the side. "So schedule him, dear. I'll butter him nicely."

"Can you handle it?"

64

"I could handle a dozen of him, believe me. Lois, you look lovely."

"Thank you, Jenny," Lois said.

"Throw me them shoes," Ida ordered.

"Jenny," George said, "is anything going to mess up the schedule? Let me know right now so I can start lying to . . ."

She stretched luxuriantly. "I'm all yours, dear. Nothing between now and the opening but all your little chores. But don't count on me for afterward. David and Matthew are coming to the opening."

George stared at her. "How did you manage that?"

She winked at him. "It wasn't easy."

"But I thought you promised . . ."

"Fix me a drink and gather round and I shall tell you of my day of adventure. It's a very old place, and sort of beautiful. Imagine, I saw the little room where David's grandfather lived when he went there. Anyway, the Rugger thing was on when we got there, and I met Matthew between halves. I should have worn Wellington boots like the other mothers. He is such a truly darling boy. They are so polite, you know. And so . . . so aware. He looks like David. I said so in front of him. That was a slip of the tongue. He informed me promptly and politely that he was adopted, and then he and David made some silly talk about dogs growing to look like their masters. They are very gruff and manly with each other, and they make odd little inside jokes."

"Did you let the boy know?" Ida asked.

"Of course not! As far as he could tell, I was one of his father's patients, and I guess he thought it a little strange his father should bring me to the school, and I could see him deciding that possibly his father was interested in me in a romantic way. All the boys in the school knew I was Jenny Bowman, of course, but I hardly ever caught them staring. They are very courteous. Matthew is dark and . . . he seems very sensitive and bright and terribly nice. If I had invented a son, he would be like that. Just like that. He was very watchful at first, but then after the game—they lost it, but Matthew said it was a good game, I really don't see how you could tell a good one from a bad one—after the game, he insisted on showing me around the school, though David wasn't exactly enthusiastic. I suppose the boy wanted to be seen with me. He was scrubbed rosy by then, and wearing his little school blazer and gray flannel trousers. And I do suppose he wanted to get to know me. It was a very special occasion for him to have his father visit him." She paused and looked indignant. "I found out that most parents get to the school three times a term, but Matthew is lucky if David visits more than once a year. Maybe I'm being unfair. They *do* seem to have a good relationship. And his Aunt Beth lives nearby and visits more often."

"So you got along with the kid?" George said.

"Marvelously! We hit it off well. We even conspired to make David climb the tower of the cathedral with us. He resented every moment of it. Two hundred and thirty-seven steps. Matthew told his father exercise was good for him. You see, the plan was that we would take Matthew to tea, drop him back at school and then David would drop me off here at the hotel. And, according to him, that would be the end of it."

"Which it should have been," George said.

She looked at him and her eyes narrowed. "I'll decide what should be and what shouldn't be, George."

"You always do."

"Don't spoil things. When we got to the top of the tower, Matthew told us he'd ordered extra tickets for us. They were doing *Pinafore,* and he was Cousin Hebe, and even David could see that it would be too cruel a disappointment for the boy if we didn't stay over to see it. So . . . we did."

"And they gave you a part," George said.

"You're trying to be nasty, aren't you? It was a good performance, really. Their voices are so clear and true. It was touching. David was beside me, and it was the voice of our son, and I had to fight to keep from crying in the wrong places. I had the feeling it was the way things should be, if David would let them be that way. And he wouldn't be shunted off like that, either. He would be home with us, where a son that young belongs. Do you know he was bundled off to boarding school when he was *eight!"*

"That's reasonably customary here, Jenny," Jason said.

"It may be customary, but it's inhuman."

"Maybe he likes it," George said.

"He has to. He hasn't much choice. Afterward there were buns and lemonade and I told him he was wonderful in the part. And I sang some of the songs with them, with my son and his friends. We practically got a whole new version going. They applauded us. I hugged him. It was the first chance I had. I held him in my arms. I . . . held him . . . close to me."

She wiped her eyes and smiled brilliantly and said, "So then I told him turnabout was fair play. I'd come to his opening, so he had to come to mine. His eyes got as big as saucers. He went running to his father and told him they were invited to my opening night. David was very surly about it. He said that Matthew was supposed to spend the first week of his holidays in Canterbury with his Aunt Beth, and then come to London for three days promised him with his father. David took me aside. He wanted to know what made me think I could break my promise about just seeing the boy once. I told him that I was not asking—Matthew was. So the Donnes, father and son, are to have the best seats in the house on Friday, George."

"Can do."

"Better do. And David was very sour on the way in. Quarrels and silences. But I do not give a damn. I wanted to see David between now and Friday. I begged him. I humbled myself. But he said no. He is a tiresome man. But on Friday night I'll sing to those two. *How* I'll sing to them!"

Jason's phone woke him at six on Tuesday morning in his room at the Dorchester. It was Wegler phoning from California, his voice slightly distorted but audible.

"Figuring the time difference, Jase, I thought this would be a good time to catch you. How are things going, my boy?"

"I would say they are going about as you expected, Sid."

"Now that isn't the happiest news in the world, is it? You remember who is picking up the tab for you, Jase. The last thing we want is to have that lovely lady, that fine property, endangering herself and a lot of other people who depend on her. I can feel a little better about this whole thing if you assure me that you are talking to her like an uncle. She respects your opinion, you know."

"I think the time for that kind of talk would have been about three or four months ago. Right now the best thing to do is to try to keep it from getting out of hand."

"Is she already in touch with him?"

"Yes. With both of them."

"How is she reacting? What is her mood?"

"Sid, I would say her mood is manic. I would say she is in a highly emotional condition. After all, it is just about the most basic emotional situation you can think of."

"Is Kogan nervous?"

"We're all nervous, Sid, and the best we can do is stand by her and help her as much as we can."

"I would hate to think that you would get a little emotional about this yourself, Jase, and help her make a damn fool of herself and ruin everything she has spent so many years building."

"I'm doing what I can, and Kogan is doing what he can. But we have a very delicate situation over here right now, Sid."

"Haven't I been telling you that?"

"You didn't tell me that Sam Dean was going to be here, nosing around." He waited for a few moments. "Hello? Sid?"

"I'm still here, my boy. That came as a blow. Does Sam Dean have any kind of a clue?"

"Not yet. But he has the idea something is wrong."

"Who gave him that idea?"

"He has a sixth sense for knowing when something is wrong. He came here from Athens. He was leaving the day after tomorrow, but he thinks he might stay and see how Jenny is getting along."

For a moment Sid's voice faded and then came back, ". . . try to keep him in the dark as long as you can, and I will try to stir up something at this end that will decoy him away from you people."

"I hope you can. We'd all feel better about it."

"The way you talk, Jase, you sound as if you were a member of that team over there. I would feel better if you sounded like a member of my team."

"I am here trying to protect your interests."

"Wholeheartedly, Jase."

"Yes indeed."

"Talk up the picture to Jenny, my boy. Tell her how well we will treat her. Tell her we are budgeting it at ten million."

"If I can get her attention."

"Speak of tax shelters, Jase. Some little things can be worked out."

"She's never been as interested in money as some of the others."

"My boy, if you can keep the roof from falling in over there, you might well be assigned to that picture for the duration."

"I would like that, Sid."

"I'll be in touch," he said and hung up.

Jason thumped the pillow and tried to find a comfortable

position and go back to sleep. But within a few minutes he knew it was no good. He kept thinking of the odd quarrel he had with Lois just before leaving their hotel. Jenny had kept them up until after one-thirty. She wanted to share the way she felt. George had kept trying to calm her down but she had resisted him. Finally she had said, her eyes blazing, "Okay, okay, okay, George! I'm a star. I'm a smash. I gave away my baby. Sam Dean is here. Okay! I'll be *careful!* I'll wear sneakers. I'll puff out my cheeks, paint myself blue and limp. But I am going to see my son again, Sam Dean or no Sam Dean, career or no career, scandal or no scandal. Now kindly shut up about it!"

"Jenny, baby, all I'm trying to do is . . ."

"All I want to be is happy," she said. "All I ever wanted to be is happy." And she began to cry. George signaled to Lois and Jason. They started toward the door. Lois paused and went over to Jenny and kissed her on the temple and whispered good night. They went out into the hall and Jason closed the door.

As Jason walked her down toward her room, Lois said, "What are we trying to do to her?"

"What does that mean?"

"George loves to wheel and deal. Ida has eighteen years of security and she's used to it. I want to see the world. You want to protect that damned picture deal. Mr. Wegler wants his star unsullied. The doctor wants her off his neck. Sam Dean wants to smash her for good." She leaned against the corridor wall beside her door and looked into his eyes, frowning. "What kind of a ride are we all trying to take at her expense, Jason?" she whispered.

"She made her choices a long time ago."

"Does that excuse you?"

"Excuse me from what, for God's sake?"

"Using her. Look how high she is? Doesn't she *know* it has to swing the other way? Doesn't she know that seeing the boy is only going to make it all worse for her?"

"Maybe she hasn't got your sense of caution, Lois."

"What do you mean by that?"

Jason shrugged. "If you gamble big, you win big or you lose big."

"And I don't gamble at all?" she asked in a strained voice.

"I didn't mean it as a criti . . ."

"I gambled big as you call it. And it only takes one big

bet to find out all the wheels are fixed and all the dice are crooked. Only a fool would keep on making bets."

"There's an old joke, Lois. It's the only game in town."

"I've heard it. It's about a compulsive gambler, isn't it?"

"Like Jenny."

"She loses, Jason. You can see that. She loses again."

"Maybe she knows that. But, you see, she had this day, didn't she?"

She looked down. "I can't make that kind of a trade, Jason. I can't trade little pieces of now for the misery of what comes after. I always see both ends of a bargain. Maybe that's my trouble." She raised her eyes slowly. "Let me alone, Jason."

"Do you think I'm the bold trader, the big gambler? My God, Lois, I live with anxiety. I know the shape and the feel of it. I hedge all my bets, and my hand shakes. I want so badly for things to have meaning that somehow I don't let them have meaning. You know, I *envy* Jenny. I get so busy worrying about what I'm doing with my life, I don't do enough with it. My history is a big long list of the things I should have done. My God, I'd trade it for a list of remorses."

"Just let me alone. Just please let me alone. Please."

She unlocked her door and went in and closed it softly. He stood there for a little while, shutting his jaw so hard his teeth ached. And then he went down the stairs instead of ringing for the elevator, walked back to his hotel in the cold night with his shoulders hunched and his hands deep in his pockets.

As he dressed he thought of the odd talk. He wondered if it could be considered a quarrel. He wondered how he should act toward her when he saw her next. He wondered if she was wondering the same thing. Perhaps they would both wait, looking for a clue. That was, he thought, the difference between them and a person like Jenny Bowman. Jenny reacted immediately, instinctively, setting the tone.

(They had waited at Jenny's hotel while Keppler viewed the last day's rushes to decide whether any final takes were necessary. And then he phoned. Jenny answered. She thanked him and hung up. And then she ran to him and hugged him with forlorn strength and put her lips against his throat and said in a small fierce voice, "Just take me a long way the hell and gone a long way away from here, just us alone and a long way, and the first plane leaving no matter where just so long as it's a warm place in the sun alone.")

He breakfasted early. There was a misty sun. He walked as far as St. James Park and sat and smoked a pipe and watched the early scurry of the civil servants heading for the complex of government buildings. He looked at the fresh young English girls and had complex fantasies born of loneliness and lust. 'See here, I don't know you and you don't know me. I may be a bit long in the tooth for you, but you look tidy and healthy and I have a four-year-old daughter who needs brothers and sisters. And you would live in California, if that sounds attractive to you. I am quiet and reasonably neat. I would be sober and faithful, and try to bring you back to England once a year to see your people. You see, my dear, people who do know each other make such a ghastly botch of it that it might be interesting to begin as total strangers.' And the young eyes would bulge and she would give him a truly frightful wallop across the chops and scream for a bobbie. He grinned. And if by any chance he did strike upon one desperate enough, heartsick enough, lonely enough to chance it, she would turn out to be slatternly and dismal, yearning for the damps of her native climate, the pubs and telly, the fish and chips, the comforting pageant of royalty. But it alarmed him to realize how vulnerable he was, that he should even entertain such a fantasy. Somehow, coming here had opened chinks in familiar armor. And a cold wind blew in.

He arrived at the Park Lane at a little after nine. When there was no answer when he phoned Lois's room, he looked in the dining room and saw her eating alone, opening mail as she ate, scribbling marginal notes on the letters. He hesitated, and when the captain of waiters started toward him, he waved him away and went to her table. He sat without invitation and as she gave him a startled look, he said, "The part of London they call The City comprises about three hundred and thirty acres. It is the part that was originally enclosed by a stone wall after the Claudian Invasion of 43 A.D. It became one of the largest and most prosperous of the Roman provincial cities. They anchored their slave galleys in the Walbrook that ran through it. The galley slaves and the enslaved inhabitants built the wall under the direction of the Roman artisans. Many parts of it are still standing, and if you have time, and if you want to get everything back into a nice historical balance, I can take you to a place where you can rest your hand against one of those stones and think of the sweat and the strain and the agony of how it was lifted into place almost two thousand years ago. When I thought I was going to get myself killed in a contemporary war I went and touched one of those stones put there by conquered men who had been children when Jesus Christ was alive."

Her gray eyes had grown wider as he spoke, her lips stretching into a smile that faded again as he finished. "Is the stone you touched still there?"

"We can go look. It was in Amen Court off Cheapside."

"It brought you luck."

"Or measles."

She shook her head. "You are a very strange man, Jason Brown."

"I wanted to tell you I don't have any idea what either of us were talking about last night."

"Thank you. And I don't remember anything I said to you. But I am going to find time to go touch that stone. Because I need luck."

"Do they make you work at breakfast?"

"A girl weeds the letters in New York and sends on batches of the ones she thinks Jenny might like to see. Then I weed them again. It has to be done sometime. And if you get too far behind, it can get very dense and nervous."

"Do they all still get answered the way they used to?"

"All except the sick ones." She looked at her watch and swooped up her coffee and finished it, scrawled her name and room number on the tab. "I've got to get up there."

"Is she up?"

"Ida promised George she would be."

"When does Sam Dean go to work?"

"We're working him in from eleven thirty to twelve, a drink and a chat up in the suite. She has to leave at twelve for lunch at the Savoy."

"Anything I can do? I feel like a fifth wheel around here."

As they crossed the lobby she said, "Come on up and check in with George anyhow."

She wore a gray cardigan, a dark skirt. There were slight shadows under her eyes. He stood next to her in the elevator, aware of her closeness and fragrance, of her tall, staunch and rounded body, and of a new flavor of closeness between them, complicated by new restraints. She would never be easy to know. It would take a long long time to know her well. There were too many defenses in depth. Too many Roman walls.

As they left the elevator he stopped her and said, "I still have one thing I think I ought to do."

"Yes?"

"She still doesn't know why I'm here."

"Don't you think she's guessed?"

"Maybe. I don't know. But I have to tell her, I think. That's the one lasting thing we had. Honesty."

Lois looked thoughtful. "Now would be the time to tell her. While she's up. But it's a brutal day, really. Ten interviews, a lunch, a dinner, two tapes."

"Any break at all?"

"From four to five. But she'll want to change and get any rest she can."

"Will you be with her all day?"

"I won't be with her at all. I have a couple hours of work to do here, plus any new stuff that may come up."

"And if I hang around?"

"I'll ignore you until the work is done, my friend."

As they walked toward the suite, George came out of his room in his shirt sleeves, a sheaf of papers in his hand. "Hey, there you are, pussycat. Morning, Jase. Add this crud to the backlog, dear. Jase, I want you in the suite at eleven twenty-five. And you too, Lois. We make it a group interview with Sam Dean."

"I think that's wise," Lois said. "Is Jenny up?"

"Up and jolly. Dressing, eating and having Gabe do her hair all at one and the same time. Not a single objection to anything on the schedule. They're all darling people. She's going to love every one of them. Even Sam."

"Well . . . good luck," Lois said. "I better get started on my stuff." She began to back away.

"Needle Harkness on that new plate. He promised to pull a proof and have it here by noon."

She nodded and turned and went down the corridor, her stride quicker than usual, dark skirt swinging, strong shoulders straight, fair hair bright in the shadows of the corridor.

"Stop panting," George said.

Jason turned and looked at George's knowing grin. "I'm way ahead of the game, boss. I get to show her a hunk of Roman wall someday."

"Get smart and she'll push it over on you," George said and went into his room. Jason followed him in.

"George," he said, "I better tell Jenny exactly why I'm here."

George started to tie his necktie. "How smart is that?"

"I'm not very smart about anything. If I was, I'd be rich. I know one thing about Jenny. She doesn't like slick tricks. The sooner I tell her the better."

"End of mission, maybe."

"Then they should have sent another boy. That's what I told Wegler in the beginning. Send another boy. I think I should tell her when she's feeling good."

George knotted the tie carefully, put his jacket on and buttoned it. "This whole thing may very probably go to hell in a bucket, pal."

"I know."

"And turn into a salvage operation. If there's anything left to salvage."

"I realize that too."

George turned from the mirror and looked steadily at him. "If it does, I want you around. Not for the salvage job. Not for picking up pieces of the career of Jenny Bowman. But for her. Can you understand that?"

"I think so. And I think you are a pretty good man, George."

"Nobody else could have picked up the pieces seven years ago. Not the pieces of the career. That was safe and sound. The pieces of Jenny Bowman." George's face twisted and darkened. He beat his fist into his palm. "All along," he said. "Right from the beginning of it all, she's deserved more than she's ever gotten. But don't tell her I said so."

"I won't."

"Four o'clock might be a good time to level with her, depending on how the day goes. Be around. I'll tip you whether it's okay."

After they left in the limousine, Jason went to Lois's room and read the *Times* while she worked. It didn't bother her to have him there. He enjoyed being near her, being able to look over and see her. She worked steadily, swiftly, making and taking phone calls, typing, stapling, filing, sending out her own letters and memos, preparing others for George's and Jenny's signatures, entering the expenses in the ledger.

At twenty after eleven, Jason walked over and stood behind her and said, "Five minute warning."

She looked at her watch. "Damn! Another fifteen minutes would have done it."

He put his hands on her shoulders and bent and kissed the nape of her neck. She froze. "Don't," she whispered.

He released her and moved away. She sat with her head lowered. "I swear I had no idea of doing that until I did it."

"Don't do things like that."

"I'm sorry."

She got up and went to a mirror and patted her hair. She fixed her mouth. She looked at him in the mirror and looked away. "Let's go," she said.

Ida was in the sitting room of the suite, mending a small tear in the silk lining of a sable cape. She had arranged bottles, glasses and ice on a small table. She moved into her bedroom and closed the door. In a few moments Jenny, George and Sam Dean arrived together. They had met in the lobby.

Jenny came sweeping in, full of a vitality that seemed to fill the room. "Lois, darling, a steep one with one rock. My God! What is my favorite color? Can you imagine that, dears? Truly a star question. A vast audience hanging breathlessly on my shy answer."

"Absolutely dead-pan she answered, 'plaid,' " George said.

"Thus sewing up the Scots," Sam Dean said.

"Sam, there's sherry for you, and probably a better brand than you deserve," Jenny said. "Are you going to ask me my favorite color? Thank you, Lois dear."

Sam Dean poured his own sherry and took the glass over to the couch. "Your favorite vice, maybe. What is it lately?"

She looked at him over the rim of her glass as she sipped her drink. She tossed her wrap on a chair. "What it always has been, darling. Recklessness. Bad judgment. Selfishness. A combination of the three. Call it Jennyism. Bowmanism. You can say I abuse the privilege of having talent. But you'd be repeating yourself, wouldn't you?"

Sam smiled. "Excellent sherry. I don't mind repeating myself. Jenny, dear, why don't you get yourself into some real gummy mess so I can have a new crusade?"

"As a special favor to you, Sam?"

"To my vast readership. Three million plus."

"What does that come to, dear. A little less than two percent of the country?"

He colored slightly. "A poor thing, but mine own."

She went over to him and sat beside him and patted his arm. "Why do we always take the knives out, Sam? I'll tell you what I'll do. I'll give you the absolute truth. Look at George! He's the color of wet cardboard."

"Don't anybody get between me and the window," George said.

"It won't make very good copy for you, Sam, because it will sound like some sort of devious plug. I'm seriously thinking of canceling out the rest of this jazzy tour. And if you put that in, it will sound like a plug for the tour. And I definitely feel squeamish about the cruddy moving picture Wegler wants me to do. Put that in and you'll be plugging the picture. But honest and truly, Sam dear, I'm bored. I've had too much of too much for too long, and I'm going stale and I want to lease an island someplace and hide for a whole beautiful year. I'm so serious about it, it's making George horribly nervous."

Sam Dean looked intently at her. "Do you mean that?"

"If you really want a nasty, you can say very accurately that my voice is going."

"Hey now!" George said.

"Shut up, Georgie. You know it. Herm knows it. I'm doing a lot of faking lately. And I've had to drop some tried and trues because the range just isn't there."

"That just isn't true, damn it!" George said.

"If I even get through this tour, I'll be astonished."

Sam Dean got up slowly and went over and poured more sherry. He turned and looked at Jenny. "Otherwise?"

"You mean aside from that? Just minor disasters, Sam. Like tax audits, nuisance suits, chronic indigestion, plane sickness, too many contracts, too big a payroll, lousy arrangements, no new songs."

Sam walked slowly back to the couch and sat beside her. He patted her arm. "And here you had me hoping you were in a real jam. Jenny darling, you've been making the same threats for years."

"But this time I *mean* them!"

"No you don't," George said soothingly.

"Don't push," she said. "You might get a hell of a shock, Georgie." She stood up. "Sam, I don't want you to feel abused, but you really didn't give us any warning, you know. I could talk to you again tonight, after midnight, if you want."

Sam finished his sherry and put the empty glass on the coffee table. His eyes were sleepy and hooded behind the thick lenses. His gold frames, tie tack, cuff links and watch band twinkled in the shadows of the sitting room.

"Thank you, darling," he said, "but it would just be for old times sake, and the old times I've given you have been bad times. I'm afraid you'll make lousy copy right now. I'll be around when you get in a real jam."

"Thanks a lot."

He got up and said formal good-bys to Lois, George and Jason. At the door he turned suddenly and said, "By the way, Jenny dear, why did you always avoid coming to London until now?"

She smiled and tapped her throat. "A batch of specialists said to keep this throat out of this climate."

"But you came here anyway?"

"I got a new batch of specialists. They said Callas thrives here."

George went out with him and closed the door. Jenny looked wide-eyed at Lois and Jason and held up both hands, her fingers crossed. Lois and Jason duplicated the gesture. They were all like that when George came back in. George slammed the door, walked over to her and hugged her and kissed her. He held her at arm's length and said wonderingly, "What's an actress like you doing wasting her time singing?"

"He bought it?"

"He said you should be on tranquilizers. I told him you ate them like peanuts. He said he wouldn't trade jobs with me for a thousand dollars a minute. He went away shaking his evil little head and muttering to himself."

"See?" Jenny said. "Trust me, George. You should always trust me. I'm really very very clever."

"You are really very very stupid, Miss Bowman. But sometimes lucky. Going to change for lunch?"

Ida came out and looked at them. She smiled. "You either fooled him or killed him. Should I look under the sofa?"

Lois put her hand over her eyes. "Not yet, Ida. Please. It's still twitching a little."

"No jury will ever convict," Ida said firmly. "I'm buying myself a drink. Any objections anybody?"

"A fast one for everybody," Jenny said. "We'll drink to crime, sin, Rugger scrums, *Pinafore* and my favorite color."

At Amen Court off Cheapside, Lois Marney said, "This stone?"

"Yes."

She touched it. She closed her eyes for a moment. "I made a wish. Is that against the rules?"

"No. That's what I did. Sort of a simple-minded ordinary wish. I wished I wouldn't get killed."

She turned and looked speculatively at him. "That isn't too entirely different from what I wished. But I can't tell you, of course."

They walked slowly along the narrow walk and out of the court. A shabby woman stared at them with a look of bleak suspicion.

"All stones are very old, of course," she said.

"But not many walls are old."

"How did you look then?"

"Thinner. A little adenoidal. Sort of hazy, I guess. Unfocused. There was a captain who kept complaining to the sergeant about the way I looked in a uniform. They all gave up, finally. They'd walk away from me, kicking at the ground and muttering."

"Were you a good soldier?"

"Except for the way I looked."

"Did you have a girl?"

"As a matter of fact, I had one right here in London. Jocelyn. And after I'd rejoined the company, she was killed here. Cued up for a movie, her father told me later, and a buzz bomb landed in the street right in front of the theater."

"How horrible!"

"By then it seemed . . . sort of remote. I told you, I was as yet unfocused. Not that I'm aimed any too damned well now."

"Did you love her?"

"I thought so."

"Do you think so now?"

"I needed her then. And she needed me. We felt very small in the middle of a war, and we tried to act as if we were born to it. But nobody is. That's sort of how I got to writing, I think. Trying to put down the essence of Jocelyn because there wasn't anything left of her. Nothing at all except what was in my mind, and that didn't seem to be enough."

"Can I read what you wrote?"

"I could never make it work."

"Will you try again some day?"

"I never thought I would. But now I think I might."

"I want to read it when you do."

"You will."

"We'll have to hurry to get you back at four, Jason."

In the taxi on the way back to the Mayfair section she seemed pensive and remote. "What are you thinking about?" he asked.

"Something you said. Twisting it around, sort of. Thinking of people feeling small in the midst of life, and trying to act as if they were born to it. But nobody is. There could be a book about that."

"Most of them are about that, Lois."

She turned and smiled at him, her mouth wry. "I get the feeling everybody is full of this terrible competence, and I'm the only one not sure of anything. But it's the same way with everybody. Even that Sam Dean. Even Jenny. But we do hearten each other, don't we? Like after Sam Dean left, everybody trying to make everybody feel things were going to be all right. And yet everything is so . . . precarious. There must be records someplace somebody could dig up. Or that doctor or Jenny could be trapped into saying the wrong thing. And then they would all come swooping down on the doctor and the boy and Jenny with their strobe lights and tape recorders, all asking questions at once, sneering and excited, and make the whole thing sickening and dirty. Then all the self-appointed moralists would write letters and make speeches about Jenny Bowman. That's the thing that would shame her and break her, because she never could explain it to them. Maybe because she can never explain it to herself, really."

He studied her. "Then what Jenny did was wrong?"

Lois scowled at him. "Of course it was wrong! You know it. She knows it. If I had a child, I would never let it go. That doesn't make me a better person. It makes me more primitive, I guess. You talk about all the pressure they put on her. The career and all. And what was best for the baby. That's all rationalization. The guilt is still in her, Jason. And that's what is driving her now. Oh, she was very good with Sam Dean, but maybe without even realizing it, she *wants* it all to come out. Maybe she's waited long enough for punishment."

"But she would be punishing the boy too."

"Has she thought it out that far?"

"She doesn't think things out. She rides on instinct, Lois."

"And dreams?"

"Yes. But what particular dream right now?"

There was a slightly contemptuous twist to Lois's mouth. "A gooey one, Jason. Famous singer abandons career to marry an old love and reclaim her son, becomes wife of noted surgeon, builds happy nest, becomes ornament in London society. What a mess of delusion!"

"Couldn't it work?"

She looked at him in astonishment. "Really, Jason! Because she might want to act out a part doesn't mean he would go along with it. And she forfeited his respect a long long time ago. What would the scandal do to his career? How long could she endure the housewife role? Six months? A year, even? And, for goodness sake, what kind of a relationship could she have with a sensitive boy once he found out she had given him away as soon as he was born? He's young enough, probably, to be hooked on the glamor of it. It is one of the daydreams of childhood to suddenly learn you're really the child of some famous person. But he would know she had rejected him, and he never would really be able to understand, no matter how carefully they explained it to him. He could understand superficially, but not in the heart, where it counts."

For a moment all the warmth of her, the capacity for indignation, compassion, understanding, was exposed, her face very alive. And then she settled back in the seat and her face became still and she retreated back into herself, as though she had spread some bright fabric before him and, when he had begun to notice it she had become aware of his attention, and had swiftly folded it, tucked it into the back of a drawer and closed it firmly and solidly.

"We should make it on time," she said in a small casual voice. She was back behind all her walls, crouched and safe.

seven

GEORGE TOLD HIM she was still in a good mood. Jason waited in the sitting room until quarter after four when Ida said it was all right to go in. Ida held the door for him and closed it behind him. The draperies were drawn. Jenny lay on the shadowy bed in a bulky white terry robe, face wiped clean of makeup, dark hair on stacked pillows. She held her hands out toward him and he went over and kissed lips that tasted soft and sweet and very young, and then sat on the edge of the bed, holding her hand.

"Recharging," she said. "Building up the batteries."

"How is it going?"

"Some of the newspaper ones are pretty fierce, Brownie. They ask questions you wouldn't believe. They try to make you mad so you'll say something they can use to make you look ridiculous. It's a strain being on guard all the time without looking as if you're on guard. Golly, it's good to have you here!"

"That's what I want to talk about."

"Honestly, Brownie, I can't really put my mind on that script. You know how I feel about things and you know what I do best. Why don't you just fake it, darling? I'll back you up on it. I love the script, really. If you see some places where you can make it fit me a little better, just change them and tell Wegler I insisted."

"It can be the best thing you've ever done."

She yawned, with a small cat-like sound. "That's what they tell me about everything, dear. This time you might be right. But I don't even want to think about it. Please."

"Wegler is very excited about having you do it. He's budgeting it big."

"Sid is an animal. Like Sam Dean. There's a pair! One big rocket. Shoot them to Mars, Pow!"

"Listen to me, honey. This isn't easy. Sid got very nervous when he heard you were starting the tour in London. The script thing is just an excuse."

Her hand closed strongly on his and her dark eyes became enormous. "Are you telling me he sent you over here to . . . to protect his lousy interest?"

"He boxed me, Jenny."

She yanked her hand away, squirmed out of the bed and stood looking down at him, her fists on her hips. "Jesus! Am I some kind of a moron? Am I some kind of an emotional incompetent? All my lousy life I get surrounded with a bunch of oily smooth-talking people, patting me on the head, telling me to be a good careful girl so they can make bigger money off me. When did you join the team, Brownie? I thought you were better than that."

"Sid knows we get along."

"Brother, we *used* to get along!"

"So he trapped me into it in such a way if I said no, I could get blacklisted for refusing to work on the script. George knows. He guessed part of it and I told him the rest. And I told him that the only thing I am interested in is what is best for you. Not what's best for me or Wegler or the industry. What is best for Jenny Bowman. He accepts that. I don't see why you can't."

She glowered down at him and chanted, "Don't be rash. Don't be foolish. Remember the stockholders. Remember your marvelous career. How many damn times have I listened to that crap?"

"Jenny, I want you to . . ."

"Let me give you a little road test, loving friend. Let me find out something. You answer one little question. Should I have gone to see the boy?"

"If you'll phrase it another way, I'll answer it."

"How?"

"Could you help going to see the boy? No. You had to. You couldn't go on any longer without seeing him. And I think David sensed that too. I think he took you out there because he knew that if he didn't, you'd find the boy on your own. And it was the only way he could hope to have any control of the situation."

She was tense for several moments, then slumped and sat beside him on the bed and began to cry quietly. He put his arm around her and held her close.

"I'm sorry, Brownie," she whispered.

"I had to come here for the wrong reasons, but I'm here. I'll do what I can. If I see you starting to do something that is going to give you pain, I'll try to stop you."

"I can't stop myself."

"I'm on your side. I always was."

She turned into his arms, put her arms around his neck and nestled close. "You make me feel safer, Brownie. I had a dream last night. I was making a stupid picture. I had to be a teen-ager, and I had to get into one of those little carts they race down hills, without motors. You know. And I stood around while they got everything ready, and then I got into the cart and they had the cameras going and they pushed me off and I started down the hill. They had extras lining the street, all bright and sunshiny and bands playing and I waved as I went by and they waved back, smiling and laughing and yelling my name. Jenny, Jenny. But then all the brightness began to blur as I went faster and faster and the hill got steeper, and as it went down, I went out of the sunlight. Into gray. There were no brakes. There weren't any people or cameras or music. Just empty gray sidewalk and the hill getting steeper and steeper and no noise but the terrible noise the steel wheels made on the cement." She shuddered in his arms.

"We won't let it be like that," he said.

"But I don't know what I'm going to do. From one minute to the next, I just don't know what I'm going to do. He's a wonderful boy. I cherish him. I've missed so much of him. So much. Golly, I'm a mess, Brownie. Like a long time ago with you."

He lifted her face. Her cheeks were streaked with tears. He kissed her salty eyes and then kissed her mouth gently. Her lips stirred. He kissed her again and suddenly her arms tightened and she responded with sudden fierce hunger, lifting to him, busying herself into a hungry readiness, ruthlessly direct, breaking her mouth against his. And suddenly she pushed herself away and said, "Whoof!" and got up and walked away. She opened the draperies, went to her mirror and looked at herself and patted her hair.

She turned and grinned at him. "Now isn't *that* all we'd need? Lest old acquaintance be forgot, or something. Nothing like an additional complication."

He laughed. "Pavlov's dogs."

"Brownie, you are a dear thing and I still love you and always will."

"Me too. But the Memory Lane thing can get overdone."

She came to him and patted his cheek and said, "And we would have felt like complete idiots. Darling, you better not come near me when I feel mimsy. You're an old familiar reflex. Anyhow, Lois would never forgive me."

He stared at her. "What the hell is that supposed to mean?"

"Dear Brownie, you two generate enough quiet tension to light a small village. Just be terribly sweet with her, please. I'm fond of her."

He shook his head. "I've made such a life work of despoiling shy maidens, I can't stop being cruel and ruthless at this late date."

"Idiot!"

"She's a very strange girl."

"She is a very sweet girl and a nice girl and a normal girl and a bright girl. She's just a little wary. Now get out of here. I forgive you for coming here to try to keep me out of trouble. But I'm through being managed. I've had it. Go on. I have to change now."

He left and went looking for George and found him in Lois's room, dictating a memo to the theater manager in Rome. When George finished he looked inquiringly at Jason.

"Forgiven," Jason said. "But a near thing for a couple of minutes."

"Good! Now we can all join hands and pray."

"If you need any historical perspective," Lois said, "Jason will take you where you can touch a lucky stone."

"If I need historical perspective," George said, "I will get quietly stoned. Sign my name to that, dear one, and get it in the mail. I'm off. You two types have yourself a fun evening."

And it was a good evening. They had quiet drinks and a good dinner, and he took her walking through the cheap neon turmoil of Soho, the narrow streets and stalls and sleazy clubs, the merged blare of rock and roll. He found to his pleasure that she was a confirmed people-watcher. She walked with her arm in his, and she would give a little squeeze with her hand when they came across the very special types. It was a good evening and an early evening, because they were both quite tired. He said good night to her in the lobby of the hotel, and watched her into the elevator until the door closed on her parting smile.

Wednesday and Thursday were busy, the tempo of appointments and interviews continuing. When Sam Dean and his companion left on Thursday, George Kogan sighed as though a yoke had been lifted from his neck. George began to give Jason small chores to do.

On Thursday, Herm Rice and Jorgenson flew back from Paris, and the whole team, including Larry, the orchestra leader, twenty-eight musicians, sound technicians and lighting technicians, stagehands and managers worked at the Palladium to put the finishing touches on the final setup.

Herm Rice, an agile, excitable gnome of a man explained it to Jason. "What we use is dynamics. Varying intensities of sound. We could go with the normal acoustics, but it cuts down on the effects you can get, right? So we set those mikes up here and three right in the band. Jenny has a walk-around mike. We get the right mix from her and the band and then blow it out of those big clusters of speakers, right? Then she can roam the whole stage and come out anyplace on the runway and it doesn't spoil the balance. And those hardwood flats under the band, they bounce it right at her to keep her timing on the button. What it is, it's live and augmented, right? We get the right mix and we get rid of any feedback anyplace she might roam to, and in the back row we can blow them out of the seats without distortion. Of course now it will sound lousy because it's pushed high on account of there'll be twenty-five hundred people soaking it up."

Jorgensen made some major changes in the runway lighting, sending Jenny back and forth, having the crew follow her with the spots. The band made the little tweedles, twangs and oomphas of tuning. Jenny wore turquoise slacks, a green sweater, white loafers and dark glasses.

Jason sat halfway back in an aisle seat beside Lois Marney. Jenny seemed very somber and intent. The way she acted reminded him of something, and when he remembered, he told Lois. He had once seen Arnold Palmer taking his first look at a golf course prior to his first practice round before a tournament. Palmer had roamed around moodily, kneeling to feel and examine the grass of fairway, rough and green, fingering the sand in the traps, throwing pinches of it into the wind, thoughtfully measuring the slopes and distances with a steady eye.

When they gave her the mike she blew into it and said, "Happy greetings to all you out there in limey land." Her voice sounded vast and hollow in the empty auditorium. "Larry, did Herm tell you 'When You're Smiling' gives him a good check off? You're set up on that? Good. Wake up the boys and tap your little foot, sweetie. Don't give me a strip-tease tempo because it's sweater weather in here. Anyhow, I don't do it. I only talk about it. Say, I like the blonde saxophone. He laughs at my jokes. Enough on voice, Herm? Okay, let's go and I'll keep moving."

The first smashing blast of the music nearly lifted Jason out of his seat. She sang. She moved, turned, roamed, strutted, her voice soaring clear and true over the slamming beat of the big band. When she finished there were conferences and discussions. Then she did "If Love Were All." And that was it. The next note she would sing on that stage would be to a full house. And to her son, and to a man she had loved.

Larry and Herm kept the band there, running them through things, checking for rough spots. Lois went back to the hotel. George sent Jason off on some minor errands. They took longer than he expected.

It was after seven when Jason returned to the Park Lane. He found George in his room, stretched out on the bed, talking on the phone. As soon as he hung up it rang again. Jason stood and looked out the window until the long conversation was over. Then he reported success with the errands. George thanked him.

"Have you got Lois sewed up, George? Or do I get to buy her a drink?"

George wore a slightly uncomfortable expression. "Better give it a rest, pal."

"What do you mean?"

"I mean let's you and me have a drink and then go downstairs and get something to eat. Okay?"

"What's the matter with Lois?"

"She's just fine, but I don't think she feels sociable. That's all. Better you should give it a rest."

"You keep saying that. Give *what* a rest? What the hell do you think I'm doing to her?"

"Now don't get sore, Jase. I guess she wouldn't want to see you for a little while."

"Don't tell me not to get sore. I am sore. What the hell has happened?"

George sat up and lit a cigarette. He glanced up at Jason. "Hell, you know how Jenny is. She's way up, but the closer it gets to curtain time, the edgier she gets. She isn't herself. You know."

"What happened?"

"We were across the hall there, and Jenny was signing some things Lois typed up for her, and Jenny started riding Lois a little, about you. She was just having a little fun with her. But . . . well, Jenny can get a little earthy sometimes. And maybe she wasn't as careful as she should have been, and she hit a nerve or something. Lois started shaking. She was white as soap. With her voice trembling she said she would appreciate it if Miss Bowman would keep her mouth off personal matters that were none of her business. Pal, when Jenny is edgy, you just don't give it to her that way. She went up like rockets. She filled that room from wall to wall. And she said a lot of things she's probably sorry for already, and sent Lois boohooing out of there on a dead run."

"How long ago was this?"

"Half an hour."

"What sort of things did she say?"

"Oh, just sort of personal things."

"Like what, George? I think you better tell me."

George looked very uncomfortable. "Well . . . like telling her she couldn't take a joke because she was scared of being a woman. She was scared of life and scared of taking any kind of a chance, and she was visibly drying up and turning into a sour prissy old maid. And she told her . . . in pretty plain language . . . just what she better do before it was too late and what would do her the most good. She said other people had made lousy marriages too. She said she was an expert on lousy marriages, but it didn't make her stop being a woman. It didn't turn her into a frozen stick. She said if one bad marriage could do that, then Lois was sick to begin with, and the marriage probably went bad because she probably acted as if the best part of marriage was something nasty. She said that if Lois really wanted to turn herself into a female eunuch, she better make one hell of a big change in the way she looks because she goes around confusing the troops."

"Dear Lord!"

"I guess it is called hitting somebody where they live. You know, nobody can hit as hard or be as sorry about it as our Jenny girl."

The phone rang and he picked it up. "Kogan. Oh, hello doll. She did? Well, I guess you better give it a little more time. I will if you want me to, but I don't know what good it will . . . Yeah, he's right here." He handed the phone to Jason and said, "Jenny."

Jenny sounded teary. "Oh, Brownie, I was lousy to her and I just called her and she hung up on me. I want to tell her I'm sorry."

"That's one thing about you, Jenny. You always say you're sorry."

"You're mad at me too."

"No. I'm not. But she's been plugging away pretty hard. You know."

"She's like family, Brownie. It was a family quarrel. I mean you say the nastiest things to the people you love. Can't you explain that to her?"

"You want me to do your apologizing?"

"You know better than that, dammit!"

"Steady, girl."

"What I want you to do, darling, is get her so she'll let me talk to her. Look, I can't have this on my mind. I have to relax. Ida gave me hell. George looked daggers at me. Now you sound . . ."

"I'll see what I can do."

"See if you can get her to come talk to me, Brownie."

"I'll see if I can get her to let you come talk to her. That would be a little more gracious, Jenny."

"I . . . I guess you're right."

He went down the corridor and tapped on Lois's door. She came close to the door and said, "Who is it?"

"Jason."

"Go away."

"Please. Let me talk to you."

After several moments the latch clicked and the door was flung open. She walked to the chest of drawers and carried a stack of clothing to the open suitcase on the bed.

"Hey! What is this?"

"What does it look like?"

He went over to a chair and sat down. "It looks like a bad time to walk out."

"She didn't leave me any choice. She was brutal and savage and vicious. Apparently anybody who doesn't share her standards is abnormal." She packed more things into the suitcase.

"Hasn't she ever climbed you before?"

She turned and stared at him. Her face was white and her eyes were reddened. "In two and a half years? Of course."

"And made you feel bad?"

"Yes."

"Why is this so different?"

"It was so personal."

"Wasn't it personal the other times?"

"Yes, Jason. But not like this. Believe me. Not like this."

"She's in tears too."

"Now isn't that just too damn bad!"

"Maybe you could stop to think that she isn't in terrific shape either right now. Her nerves are pretty well shot."

"She seems happy enough."

"You're leaving George in a hell of a spot."

"I'm sorry about that. I told you, though. She left me no choice. She said those things in front of George and Ida. I can't face any of them again. Do you know what she said?"

"I've got a general idea. Lois, honey, why . . ."

"Don't *honey* me! All you people cheapen everything."

"All us bawdy, rancid showbiz types?"

"Not you, Jason. I'm sorry I said that."

"Will you do one thing for me?"

"Like?"

"Give her a chance to say she's sorry."

"I don't want to see her again. It won't do her the least bit of good."

"At least she'll be able to say she tried to patch it up."

"Why should I do that much for Jenny Bowman?"

"Because you'll always wish you had, Lois. You have a nasty streak of fairness in you."

She hesitated and said, "Well . . . it won't do any good, but if she wants to come here and apologize, I'll at least listen to her."

He went back to the suite. Jenny looked strained and unhappy. "She'll listen to you but she says it won't do any good. She's packing."

"Ida said she would be. I didn't believe it. Gee, I was awful, Brownie."

"You're a star. And I think you're going to need all the talent you've got."

Jenny hurried to Lois's room. George came wandering in, glass in hand. Jason told him Lois was packing. George sat down limply and hit himself in the forehead with the heel of his hand. They waited. They had drinks and they waited.

A half hour. Forty-five minutes. An hour. An hour and twenty minutes.

Jenny drifted in. She stopped and stood, swaying slightly, wearing a beatific smile. She focused on them with apparent effort. "Scoun'rels all of you," she said in a dreamy voice. "Anything in pants, classified as rat. No. Everything wears pants. Even pork chops. Anything that can grow a beard, basically rat."

"Jenny love," George said, "you are smashed."

"Mmmm," she said.

"How's Lois?" Jason asked.

"Equiv . . . equivalently smashed."

"What happened?"

She aimed herself vaguely at the bedroom door. "Happened? Oh, we hugged and cried and talked about broken hearts. Men are lousy. Boy, what a stinker she stuck with for too long. And, here and there, to and fro, round and about, we had us a couple little knocks. Where's Ida? Oh, there you are! Sweety bun, see if you can get a steak into me before I fall asleep."

As she disappeared into the bedroom, George yelled, "Is Lois leaving?"

She stuck her head back out and gave him an owlish look. "Leaving? Where she want to go. She wants to go out and hell around, count me out, please. I am a very tired girl. Very very tired." She shut the door.

"Best thing in the world," George said contentedly. "She'll sleep around the clock. She'll sleep right through the hangover. Tomorrow night she'll swing. Ready to go eat, Jase?"

"I think I'll check on Lois."

"I'm not about to wait for you, pal."

Jason went back down the hall. Lois's door was ajar. He pushed it open and called her name. She made a strangled sound. He went in and found her sitting on the low sill of an open window, holding her head out into the night air. He ran to her and took hold of her shoulder.

She looked up at him with an agonized expression. "Laid down and the bed went around and around. Oh, Jason, I feel terrible!"

He found flat-heeled shoes and put them on her. He put her jacket on. He hung her tweed cape around her shoulders. He found the room key and put it in his pocket. As he walked her out the door she said, listlessly, "Where we going?"

"To get you some air."

"Don't let me fall down. Please don't let me fall down in front of anybody."

"I won't let you."

He got her down in the elevator and out through the lobby without incident. It was a misty night, the street lamps haloed. He put his arm around her waist under the cape and walked her down Park Lane to Piccadilly and west on Piccadilly. He set a reasonably fast pace. Her round hip bumped clumsily against him. He felt the stretch of the warm muscles of her slender waist against his hand. The mist made droplets in her shining hair. He could hear her taking deep breaths.

"Drink to trying to understand each other," she muttered, "and then drink to getting to understand each other, and drink to really understanding each other."

"Do you?" Jason asked.

"She's a lovely lovely person," Lois said solemnly. "She's a lovely *sad* person. She's had a sad terrible wonderful life."

"Yes she has."

"But things happening. You know? Enough crammed into one life for three or four people. She really really knows she's alive."

"She's as alive as anybody I've ever known."

"You're right! You're so right!" She stopped suddenly and turned and faced him. She put her hands on his shoulders and looked at him with an almost cross-eyed intensity. "You are specially sweet. You know? She told me that. We cried because you are especially sweet, Jason Mason. Of everybody to be scared of, not you. Huh? Do you want to unscare me?"

"I want to walk you, Lois."

"Hah!" she said. "Pretty dull proposition. Okay. Walk me. Walk me good."

As her coordination began to improve, he lengthened his stride, and soon she no longer needed his arm around her. She began to swing along adequately, holding her chin high, taking deep breaths. He walked her down to The Mall, around the Victoria Memorial and back Constitution Hill and started her down Grosvenor Place. She kept the pace grimly and silently for a long time and finally stopped and walked over and leaned against a wrought-iron fence and said faintly, gasping, "What are you trying to do to me anyway?"

"How do you feel?"

"Well . . . offhand, I feel persecuted."

"Do you feel sober?"

"I think so, Jason. I have a very ugly little headache right smack between my eyes, and my mouth tastes foul, and I don't really think I can walk another step. What time is it?"

"Quarter after midnight."

"Have I made a terrible fool of myself?"

"People seldom go through the lobby of the Park Lane on their hands and knees."

"Oh my God!"

"No, Lois. You were fine. Really."

She looked at him, wan in the night lights, "Did I say any strange things to you?"

"No."

"I like that crumply old hat you wear."

"It's a new hat. The day after I buy them, they look like this."

"I'm not drunk but I feel silly. Even with a headache and a bad taste I feel silly."

"Now we take the next steps, Lois. Coffee, supper, wine, and a slow walk and good night."

"Do you have the steps written out on a little card?"

"At this hour the food thing may need a little organizing. Come on, and we'll find a phone."

"Will my legs work?"

"Let's find out."

He found one of the ludicrously ornate public phone booths, got Tommy Bird's card out of his wallet, phoned Tommy's residence number and stated his problem. As he talked, Lois leaned against the glass and peered in at him. Tommy was professionally affable, gave him an address on St. James Street and said he would phone ahead. Anything Jase wanted, anything at all, just pick up the phone any time, buddy.

It was a private club. He spoke into a tube. The latch buzzed and he pushed the door open and they went up to the second floor. It was all very hushed and luxurious and courteous. They were ushered to a small private dining room where candles burned on a table set for two. It was more like a small apartment than a dining room, with low lamps, a broad low couch, lavatory, gentle music piped in at an almost inaudible pitch. It was rather more than Jason had anticipated. When the waiter took the coffee order and went softly out and closed the paneled door, the tiny click of the latch made Lois leap slightly, like a doe hearing a gun being cocked. She went into the bath. She was still in there when the coffee came. The waiter knocked at the door and waited permission before opening it.

"When you are ready to order, sir, if you would press the button beside the door, sir."

"Thank you."

The waiter leaned a bit closer. "There is bedding, sir, in the cabinet at the foot of the couch."

"Uh . . . thank you. I don't think we will need . . ."

"Mr. Bird asked that you be made comfortable, sir."

"Everything is fine. Just fine," Jason said heartily.

"Very well, sir," the waiter said and glided out.

Lois came out in a few moments. She looked wary and jumpy. She slid into the chair opposite his and he poured her coffee. Her hair was brushed to a silken gleam in the candlelight, the diagonal bangs lying evenly across her smooth brow.

She sipped her coffee and said, "I don't think I'm hungry."

"You should eat."

"I think I better drink this and you take me home."

"I think you ought to try to eat."

"Jason . . . what kind of a place is this?"

"Listen to me, Lois. Look at me. I know what it looks like. I know what you're thinking. I swear to you, I asked Bird to tell me a good place to have supper at this hour, and I said I had a lady with me. And that is *all* I said."

The gray eyes stared at him, slightly narrowed. And then she smiled and gave a little nod and said, "I am ravenous! I could eat the tablecloth and the candles."

They had very thick slices of rare roast beef, steaming baked potatoes with chives and sour cream, icy lettuce with oil and wine vinegar, a bottle of a rich and full-bodied Burgundy. They ate with hunger and talked well. She was flushed and relaxed, her face softened, her eyes unguarded. They seemed to be able to make each other laugh very easily. The candles dwindled and the music was an unobtrusive background. She was a very lovely woman, and when she forgot her tensions her voice was softer, and lower in pitch.

But ten minutes after the last of the food and the wine was gone, they both started to say something at the same time. They paused, did it again, laughed, and unexpectedly all the constraint was back.

He sought to break it. "We're important, Lois. Do you sense what I mean? Of no importance to the world at large. But together . . . something special."

"This is bigger than both of us?" she said acidly.

"You knew about touching the stone. You know about a lot of things."

"If you buzz for that little man, we can pay him, Jason."

He hesitated. "Of course," he said. He got up and walked toward the door.

"Jason?" her voice was strained and thin. He turned and looked at her. She stood up and came to him, looked frightened and white and sacrificial. She stood close to him and closed her eyes. He put his arms around her. Her lips were cold and compressed. Her body was taut and tremorous. She rested her hands on his shoulders, slack-wristed, as light and unemphatic as a touch of bird wings.

"I'll take you home," he said.

"If you give me a little . . ."

"It's very late. I'll take you home."

She backed away. "Too late, perhaps."

"Perhaps."

The waiter came. He said they were Mr. Bird's guests. When Jason reached for pound notes, he said gratuities were not permitted. They went down the stairway and out into the chilly empty street. He strolled her up to Piccadilly and west to Park Lane. She walked silently beside him for a long time. At last she took his arm and said, "Forgive me. I'm such a damned mess."

"You're fine, Lois."

"Oh, sure. So many of the things Jenny said were true. That was what made it so bad. But . . . I am what I am. Like . . . a damned big bowl of waxed fruit. You see, I had to teach myself not to respond. That was the hold he had. And I had to break it. And I taught myself too good. When finally there was nothing he could do that meant anything, when I could feel absolutely nothing at all, then I was free of him. It was survival, Jason. I had to fight for it. Otherwise I was lost forever. It . . . it's the price I paid, I guess. And it's the bargain I have to live with."

"I can understand."

"Such a strange thing to do to oneself," she said. "I was so much one way, and then I turned myself into the complete opposite. It's as if I broke something. Or more like a machine, and you just take out one little wheel and lose it, and it doesn't work any more."

"We believe we're so very very stabilized and functional," he said, "until something happens and we find out that the whole mechanism was in a very precarious state of balance all the time. I thought I could always work, no matter what. I could do the hack jobs, rough carpentry on scripts. Thank God I'd been reasonably bright about money and taxes. After Joyce died, I'd put paper in the machine and I couldn't even write, 'I see the cat.' I'd look at the paper and my stomach would knot up and my vision would blur. I tried a hundred little tricks. I copied whole books. I copied old stuff I'd written. But I couldn't make up a new sentence. I couldn't even write letters to friends. One year and four months it went on. I cashed in everything I'd put aside. I lost my reputation for reliability. Then one day it started again. A little bit on the slow side. But it started."

"What started it?"

"Bonny. I could tell her bedtime stories. I could make them up. She loved one, about an Easter bunny who hated eggs. She made me tell it over and over. One night I made myself write it down. In longhand. The sweat poured off me. The next morning I could hardly read that scrawl, but I copied it on the typewriter and made some small improvements, sweating as before. The following day I was all right. But it shook me. It gave me a dose of humility. I learned that it *could* happen. Ever since, I run just a little bit scared. Because, after all, it's the only work I know."

The hotel lobby was empty. He walked her to the elevator, took her hand. She said it had been a wonderful evening, and could not quite meet his eyes. She got in and it started up. Suddenly he remembered the key. Just the one lift was operating at that hour. He hurried to the stairway and went up the stairs, two at a time, to the third floor. He met her coming along the corridor. She gave a start of surprise. He held up her room key.

"How silly," she said. "I didn't even know I didn't have it."

He walked to her room and unlocked the door for her and swung it open. She turned toward him in the doorway of the dark room, and he gave her the key. She looked at him and he took her in his arms. Her mouth was soft and warm and responsive, as once before on that first rainy night. She tried momentarily to break away, but he held her close. He ran his hand up the flat strength of her back to the silken nape of her neck. He worked her back into the darkness of the room, caught the edge of the door with his elbow and swung it shut. She began to pant, and her breath made a soft rasping sound in her throat.

"Don't let me," she whispered. "Oh, please, don't let me. Don't."

But there were the kissings and the touchings, furnace breath and the slow and fumbling and entwined passage back to the dark bed. And she, in whines and sobs, in beggings and broken protestings, alternated her expressions and acts of hunger that grew ever more insistent, with constraints and escapes and evasions which dwindled in force and frequency. She half helped and half hindered him as he fumbled her clothing off, gasping and shuddering, but when all of it was gone and he lay with her, and kicked the half-packed suitcase off to thud onto the floor, she was then beyond reserve or restraint. She was then a long strong heated woman, full of the restless sighing movements of her need, firm of breast, soft and muscular in belly and hips, greedy with lips and hands, moaning her love words, writhing in a slow deep luxury of her need, calling his name over and over.

It was very fierce and quick, and there was a resting time, soothing and murmurous, entwined and safe, and then there was a longer time for them, lasting and steady and very complete, bringing the sleep upon them quickly. He awoke when the room was gray with the first light. They were under the covers, and she was at the far edge of the bed, her back toward him, her shoulder bare, her pale hair clotted and tousled. At first he thought she was making some strange smothered sound in her sleep, and soon he realized she was weeping.

He reached and put his hand on her shoulder and said, "Darling?"

She shrugged his hand off violently. "Go mark your score card," she said in a constricted voice.

"What are you talking about?"

She turned and sat up, holding the covers against her breast, staring down at him with an angry, tear-stained face. "You did fine, didn't you? You made out. Go tell them you took the necessary therapeutic measures, you bastard!"

"Now wait a minute, darling."

"I'm not your darling, Mr. Brown. Were you following Jenny's suggestion? Go and smirk and wink at them all. Mission accomplished. You polished off the stone butterfly."

"Now, *hold* it!"

"You suckered me with old materials. Candlelight, wine and sweet words. Soft music, even. Was it violins? I didn't notice."

"Lois, you don't . . ."

"That little trick with the room key was particularly good. I congratulate you. You're a very careful and clever planner, Jason."

He sat up and faced her. "You're sick," he said.

"Really? You know, I don't feel the least bit sick. Do you know how I feel? How I really and truly feel? I feel dirty!"

With remote and objective awe he saw his arm swing up and saw his palm crack across her cheek. The tears burst out of her. She scrambled out of her side of the bed. She stumbled on the suitcase. She ran around the end of the bed and ran to the bathroom, her strong and beautiful figure luminous in the dawn light. They really shouldn't run, he thought. They shouldn't ever run unclad. She banged the door behind her and locked it.

In a little while, after looking wonderingly at the palm of his hand, he got up and trudged to the bathroom door. He heard her sobbing in there. He tapped on the door.

"Go away!" she wailed.

He picked up her clothing and placed it neatly on the chaise. He got dressed. He put on his topcoat. He put his hat on the back of his head. He stared around the room. He went over to her typewriter, uncovered it and rolled a clean sheet of paper into it. There was just enough light to see the words. He wrote a few complex things of protestation, clarification, explanation—all conditional phrases. He tore them out and crumpled them and shoved them, one by one, into his topcoat pocket. And finally he called on what he thought he knew of women, and what little he could guess of what was wrong with her, and what he felt toward her.

If the four words could do nothing, then there was nothing which could be done. I DO LOVE YOU, he wrote, in capitals, and rolled it up a few spaces and left it in the machine. He walked to his hotel, damning all varieties of neurosis, had a hot tub and slept deeply until noon.

During the late afternoon turmoil prior to the opening, he

saw Lois for a few brief moments when she brought some papers to George Kogan's room. She gave him a fleeting gray glance, murmured a muted greeting. Her eyes were dark smudged and downcast. She had the limpid gravity of a madonna, and moved as though something very fragile were balanced on her head. She closed the door behind her without a sound.

"Everything seems to be all right?" Jason asked heartily.

"If we can get the damned ticket thing straightened . . ."

"I mean with Lois."

"With Lois? Oh, sure. Everything is fine. Just fine."

"That's nice."

Jason Brown walked out onto the stage of the Palladium. The big band was in rehearsal clothes. George Kogan was at the standing microphone. They were adjusting the lights on him. The band hit a loud driving beat. "I saw you there, one wonderful day . . ." George sang, snapping his fingers, tapping his feet to the rhythm. He made a face at Jason. An electrician brought him the walk-around mike. George moved over toward Jason, singing, "That's why I asked the Lord in Heaven above, what is this thing—called love." He turned and advanced to the footlights and conducted with waving arms the last few driving bars of the number, singing, "Love! Love! Love! Love! Love!"

George grinned and made a thumb and finger circle and called down to Larry, "You've done it again, Larry."

Behind Jason, the theater manager came to the wings and said, "She's leaving the hotel."

"Jolly good," George said.

"You've got fifty-five minutes, gentlemen," Larry said to the orchestra.

George handed the mike to the electrician and walked slowly toward the wings with Jason. "How is she?" Jason asked.

George shrugged. "Like always. Wound up tight. Babbling around. You know. All of a sudden London is her favorite town. Her lucky town. Dear warm people. She could settle down here."

"With the doctor?"

"That's what Ida said. And added one of her sayings. If at first you don't succeed, don't try again. It saves wear and tear. Jenny wasn't impressed."

"She's never taken that kind of advice."

"Any advice, pal."

In the dressing room corridor a telegraph boy came up to them and asked which one was Mr. Kogan. He handed the wire to George. Jason saw that it was addressed to Jenny. George thumbed it open. He was walking slowly. He stopped as though he had run into a wall. "Oh brother!" he said.

"What's the matter?"

George handed him the wire. It was signed David Donne. It was a very polite and proper message. It wished her success on her opening night. It said a medical emergency had come up. It expressed regrets. Jason handed it back and George put it in his pocket.

"She just might not go on."

"You don't mean that."

"She's been bracing herself for a special audience, and if it isn't there it's like no audience at all. I think I better save this until after. Come on, let's get some air."

"It's raining out there, George."

"With a little luck, maybe we can drown."

They went out the stage door and down the alley to the street. It was not too wet close to the building. The front of the theater was brightly lighted. Heavy traffic was inching along the street. Crowds were milling around the outer lobby waiting to be admitted to the reserved seats, moving around the huge cutout photograph of Jenny and around the placards announcing HOUSE FULL. Down the alley on the other side hundreds of people waited in line, four abreast, waiting for gallery seats, and being entertained by a group of buskers singing comedy songs and wearing strange bonnets. It was a festival scene, full of excitement and anticipation.

"The world of Jenny Bowman," George said, raising his voice over the hubbub.

"Isn't that the car?"

"Where? Yes. If they can get through. A jam like this will pick her up good."

Jason could see them in the car as the policemen cleared a path so the car could turn into the lane to the stage door. Jenny was smiling out at the crowd through the rain-streaked window with the surprising innocence of a delighted child. Ida sat beside her. Gabe, the hairdresser, and Lois were on the jump seats.

Jason followed George back to the stage door. The stage door keeper came out with an umbrella and opened it.

Jenny stepped out and said, "What are they giving away in there? Did you see them out front, George?"

"Mounted policemen. You can't rate any higher."

"Hello, Charlie. Sorry to bring you out on such a bad night."

"No trouble at all, Miss Bowman."

She started toward the door, stopped and said, "George, are you sure you . . ."

"I am sure I left two prime tickets at the box office plainly and unmistakably marked, just like I told you the last . . ."

"Wuff wuff," she said and winked and went in.

Lois and the hairdresser and Ida followed along. The theater manager was greeting Jenny as Jason followed George in. "Good evening, Miss Bowman! Good evening! A rainy night but a wonderful audience."

They could hear the distant murmurous sounds of the audience entering the theater.

The manager escorted Jenny along the corridor to the dressing room. Gabe and Lois followed along. Lois had given Jason another of those muted glances, a look he could not read. It did not seem angry or hurt or even inquisitive. It seemed more speculative. A measuring. She carried a bulky dispatch case. As Ida started to follow them, Jason saw George draw her aside and show her the wire. Ida swallowed hard and made a soundless whistle. George murmured something to her and she nodded and hurried on to catch up with Jenny.

George beckoned to Jason. "Come join the happy throng, pal."

"Is there room for us and the flowers too?"

"There's always room."

They passed the manager heading away from the dressing room, smiling and rubbing his hands together. George rapped once and opened the door. The room was banked with flowers. Ida was carrying Jenny's glittering gown in its Pliofilm wrap into the screened dressing area. Jenny was leaning toward the dressing table mirror, poking gingerly at the corner of her mouth. Lois sat in a corner leafing through the accumulated wires and cables.

"My lucky town, George," Jenny said. "Rainy old luck-town."

"They'll all lucky, Jenny-cat."

"Cable from Wegler," Lois said.

"How terribly terribly sweet! He must expect to make money on me somehow."

"He's entering you in the fifth at Pimlico," George said.

"Tonight I'd make it by six lengths. I feel GOOD!"

"A cute one from Biddy in New Delhi," Lois said. "It says: 'TO ALL YOUR LUCK LOOKS TALENT AND MONEY AND MOSTLY YOUR MONEY DEAREST.' "

"Tonight, dears, I have the luck and uncle has the money. George, did David pick up his tickets yet?"

George hesitated. "I'll check it out."

"You do that," she said and went into the dressing area. The hairdresser laid out a few small tools on a table near the dressing table bench. From the dressing area she called, "George, you tell Brownie exactly where those seats are. Brownie, your job is to grab those two and hustle them right back here the moment I have given my all. Use those mounted cops if you have to. But bring them."

"That I will."

"Just look for the nicest boy in town, and one of the handsomest men."

"There's about ten here you should look at later, I think," Lois called.

"Thank you, dear."

"I have to go check the standing room tally," Lois said to George. "Should I find out about those two tickets for you?"

"Please," George said cheerfully. As she went out the door, George looked meaningfully at Jason, patted the pocket where the wire was and motioned with his head toward the closing door.

Jason hurried out and caught up with her in the corridor. "Lois!"

She kept walking. "Really, I'm too busy to . . ."

He caught her by the arm and stopped her. "I have a message from George."

"Wishing us luck? You're full of tricks."

"Shut up a minute. A wire came from the doctor. They aren't going to make it."

She looked directly at him, her eyes widening. "Oh, *no!*"

"So George is going to tell her it came after she was on. I guess he wants a united front. Ida knows."

"It will break her heart."

"You did get my message."

"Please let go of my arm. I have lots to do, Jason."

"Can't you say *anything*?"

She pulled away from him. "What could I possibly say? You made a fool of me. You got what you were after. Let's leave it at that."

"I can't leave it at that."

"I wouldn't say you had much choice," she said and walked away.

He looked at her erect walk, the severe shoulders, the shining head, the constrained sway of her skirt. He resisted the temptation to drive his fist into the wall beside him. He roamed into the backstage areas, the gloom smelling of dust and insulation. He found a place where he could look diagonally out. The stir and buzz of the throng seemed much louder there. The footlights were on and he could see nothing beyond them. He heard some furtive tweedles, a muted paradiddle on the snare and now the band was in place. In the center of the huge stage Jenny's microphone stood alone, in a circle of light.

He went back to the dressing room, knocked once in George's fashion and went in. Jenny was at her dressing table applying her makeup. Gabe was working on her hair. She smiled brilliantly at Jason in the mirror and said, "Am I gorgeous? Am I breathtaking?"

"Fabulous," Jason said.

"You're using my word," George said.

The smile faded and she looked nervously at Jason. She got up and turned toward him like a child inviting inspection. Gabe moved behind her to continue on her hair. "All right really?" she asked anxiously.

He stepped to her and kissed her lightly on the forehead and said, "*Very* much all right, Jenny Bowman." The anxiety faded.

(In the little suite in the Del Prado he had seen her stare at herself in helpless, unjustified disgust. "So little to go on," she had said. "I'm a leggy, willowy, hollow-cheeked blonde at heart. Trapped here in this sort of dumpy little broad with a wide little-kid face." He had tried to convince her she was lovely. And she was. But it was a basic insecurity with her, enmeshed with a lot of other little knots and webs of insecurity. He had begun then to tell her more often how much he loved the way she looked, and he saw it help her in the way he wanted to help her. It made no sense. But it was something she needed.)

"Jenny darling, should we start the overture?" George asked.

"How about those tickets?"

"I don't know yet. They're pretty jammed up out there. And traffic is pretty heavy. It's ten minutes to. A lot of them will be making it at the last . . ."

"Call the box office again, George."

Ida cleared her throat. "Like George says, it's a madhouse out there."

George opened the door, trying to entice Jenny out. "It's the price of popularity, darling."

She took a step and then stopped and looked at their tense faces.

"What is it?" she demanded.

"What is what, honey?" George asked, just a little too blankly.

"Something is going on and I want to know what it is!" she said, staring intently at each of them in turn.

"Jenny," George said, "you know me. Whatever I know you know. Just don't get upset."

"I'm not upset, but I may get upset, *very* upset, unless you tell me *what's going on!*" Her jaw was set, her eyes hard and blazing.

George hesitated, started to speak, and then shrugged and sighed and took the telegram out of his pocket and handed it to her. She read it swiftly and then turned away from them.

George said, "Jenny, I know this is a big disappointment . . ."

"But he *said* he was coming . . ." she said in a stifled voice.

"Darling, you were hoping to have twenty-five hundred out there tonight. But all you get is twenty-four hundred and ninety-eight. That's still a lot of people. What do you say? Shall we start the overture?"

"But he *promised*," she said with tears in her voice.

The commissionaire appeared in the doorway. He looked upset. "There is a Mr. Donne here, Miss Bowman, who insists that you . . ."

She whirled, her face alight, tears standing in her eyes. "Oh, show him in, please!"

A boy appeared in the doorway, a slender boy, not tall but with the look of tallness to come. He was hesitant, but poised, neat in his dark suit, tie perfectly knotted, dark hair brushed. Jason saw the trace of Jenny in his face, in the shape of brow, directness of eye, stubborn delicacy of chin.

"Hello, Matthew," Jenny said with a warm and wonderful smile, going to him.

He put his hand out and said, "Hello, Miss Bowman."

"How nice you look! Come in, come in." She kissed him and led him into the room. "Matthew, these are my good friends. Miss Ida Mulligan. Mr. Gabe. Mr. George Kogan. Mr. Jason Brown. This is Mr. Matthew Donne, of Canterbury School."

The boy acknowledged the introductions very correctly, looking directly at each of them, repeating the names. He looked at the masses of flowers and looked with a slightly owlish humor at Jenny. "Not a bit like Canterbury opening night, is it?"

Jenny seemed distracted. She kept glancing at the empty doorway. "How did you get here, Matthew? Is your father here?"

"I expect you got the telegram? It was a call from Italy, Miss Bowman."

"You promised to call me Jenny."

The boy smiled. It was a good smile, direct and aware. "I expect I should, if I promised. But it does seem a bit pushy. Jenny, then. It was an emergency case, someone quite important I imagine. Do you know, they've sold off all the standing room too?"

Jenny straightened her shoulders. "George?"

"Yes, Jenny."

"Start the overture."

George grinned and hurried out. Ida and Gabe advanced on Jenny and began small, final, unnecessary adjustments. The boy gave Jason a rather uncertain smile and backed out of the way.

"Was it all right, my coming alone?" he asked.

Jenny gave him warm and immediate reassurance. "It was more than all right. I'm very much complimented. I'm delighted. I would have been terribly disappointed if you hadn't. Now come along with me, dear."

Ida and Gabe remained behind. Jason followed Jenny and her son to the backstage area. He heard the overture begin.

Jenny turned to Jason and said, "Brownie, would you please see that . . ."

"Miss Bowman. Jenny," the boy said. "I guess I should tell you. Actually, I came up to town on my own. They don't know I'm here."

Jenny looked at the boy with an odd expression. "Your father doesn't know?"

"I imagine he thinks I'm in Canterbury with Aunty Beth." Jason said, "Might be a good idea to let her know."

"Yes, of course," Jenny said with a distracted frown. Lois came up to them at that moment and was introduced. When she heard the boy's name, she gave Jason a quick, questioning look.

With a sudden intensity, Jenny put her hand on the boy's shoulder and said, "I know what we'll do. Your father stood us both up tonight, dear, but we're not going to let that get us down. After the show, you're going to have supper with me, and then we're going to bed you down at the hotel, and we'll spend tomorrow together."

The boy looked pleased but worried. "That would be very nice, but I'm afraid Aunty Beth would positively . . ."

"Lois will explain it very nicely to Aunty Beth, won't you, Lois?"

"I'll try. How do I get in touch with her, Matthew?" Lois said.

"It's Miss Nevison," the boy said and gave Lois the Canterbury phone number. "Thank you so much! I do hope they won't be too cross about it."

"They may be jealous," Jenny said, "but I don't think they'll be angry. Lois, dear, would you turn this young man over to one of the ushers, please? You do have your ticket, Matthew?"

"I picked it up at the box office. I explained to them they might sell the other one, and they did so, very quickly."

Jenny laughed. "You can be my assistant business manger, dear."

The boy held his hand out. "I hope it goes very well, Jenny."

She kissed him again, and the boy looked slightly uncomfortable. "Having you here is going to make it go well. And your father is going to be awfully sorry he missed it."

Jason saw Jenny look at the boy as he went off with Lois. He saw the softness and the pride and the yearning in her eyes. Then she moved slowly to the corner of the stage. Jason waited, several feet behind her. George suddenly appeared beside him. Jason sensed another presence and turned and saw Ida.

Jenny stood, and Jason could sense the way she was letting the music take her. She was opening herself, letting the music move into her, letting it push everything else back into a far corner of her mind, letting it take her and build her into the public Jenny Bowman, the performer, totally keyed to the music, to the audience. At the right cue, as the big band shifted smoothly into a faster and more insistent rhythm, Jenny seemed to grow, to take on more stature, to become more vivid and electric, her eyes shining, foot tapping, body moving in tempo. The audience anticipation was a tangible thing. The back of Jason's neck and the backs of his hands tingled. George wore a broad maniacal grin and his face was flushed. The band went into her introductions. She reached a hand back without looking. George slapped the walk-around mike into it, and she walked swiftly out into the great crash of applause, smiling, vibrant, meeting the applause and then taking charge with the opening bars of her opening song, *"I Could Go on Singing."*

She took it from the back of the big stage first, all that music and that big voice filling the great theater like a huge earthen bowl filled to the brim with quicksilver. And as she built to the climax she went out onto the runway that took her out over the audience. She built it hard and true, pulling the band with her into a drive never achieved in rehearsals, and ended it with a punch that seemed to lift the whole audience out of their seats.

Amidst the shocking roar of applause, George hammered Jason on the back and jumped up and down and yelled, "She's got it tonight! Oh, man, she's got it all tonight!"

eight

AT TEN THIRTY on Saturday morning, Jason tapped on the door of Lois Marney's room. She opened the door, said a toneless, expressionless good morning and went back to her typing. He dropped his topcoat and hat on the chaise and went and stood looking out the window, hands in his hip pockets, unlit pipe clenched between his teeth.

The sound of typing stopped. "George is with the recording people," she said.

"So Ida told me. Have any trouble with the aunt?"

"She's an old lady. The boy told me she has a very strong will. She wasn't exactly pleased. She wasn't at all certain she'd ever heard of Jenny Bowman. And she doesn't seem to think entertainers are reliable people. It took a long time to reassure her."

"When does the boy go back?"

"On a train early this afternoon, I think."

"She got a room for him all right?"

"It connects with the suite. They moved somebody." She frowned. The morning light slanted across her. She wore a dark blue wool dress with a plain neckline. She looked very lovely and withdrawn and unapproachable. "The aunt asked a very shrewd question, Jason. Why? It is a good question, isn't it?"

"Embarrassingly good."

She leaned back in her chair and looked at him. "And the boy is asking it too, I think. I *like* that boy. He has those wonderful manners and all that poise, but he isn't a little prig. He's very bright and aware. He knows Jenny is a friend and a patient of his father. But she's also a celebrity. Why should she give so much time and attention to an English schoolboy?"

"Because she likes him."

"That might be enough for the boy. The aunt isn't quite satisfied. And I guess we can be glad Sam Dean left when he did."

"There are other reporters."

"She wore my raincoat and a scarf over her hair. I guess she senses it's smart to be inconspicuous. And it gives her and the boy more privacy."

"Did they leave early?"

"By nine, I think. Ida said the boy was talking about some sort of excursion boat that goes up and down the river, so she could see London. Can you imagine Jenny as a tourist?"

"If she's with the boy, everything will please her."

"She's trying to charm him," Lois said.

"Of course."

"Is that entirely honest, Jason?"

"It's entirely Jenny."

He moved closer to the table, leaned against it and looked down at her. She looked away, blushing slightly.

"Lois. We have to talk."

"Do we?"

"You can't just wall it off, like everything else."

The flush faded to pallor. She looked at him and her mouth was compressed. "There's some mythology about these things, isn't there? You caught me off guard, and you made me react. You certainly made me react, didn't you? All the way. And according to male mythology, that's supposed to turn me to putty in your hands, isn't it? Some sort of a damned swooning conditioned reflex. But I'm not following the rules. Is that why you keep looking so baffled? I *resent* what happened, Jason. I resent the invasion of privacy. No pun intended. I resent what it does to my pride and my self-respect. You had no right. I'm not a thing. I'm a woman. I'm not something you can just walk up and use like that. You did, and I let you, and I shouldn't have. And I won't again. I've slammed all the doors, Jason."

He looked at her in anger. "You have a very basic part of it wrong. It makes me out some kind of a damned goat. I don't have hooves and smell of brimstone, for God's sake! What seems to escape you, Lois, is any slight idea that it might have been something I thought very meaningful to both of . . ."

"Like you said in your little message? You do love me? Oh come now, Jason. Really! Isn't that the next gambit? This is bigger than both of us? Isn't that the way you rationalize it and hope I will, so you can convince me we should keep on with it? Aren't we a little too grown up for that? It was a dreary little episode between a couple of relative strangers,

Jason. And nothing we can say can turn it into some sort of glowing emotional experience."

He looked at her wonderingly. "You're really as cold as a fish, aren't you?"

"Challenging me? I already proved I'm not physically cold. I don't have to prove it again, thank you."

"Emotionally cold, Lois."

"Emotionally realistic. Come now, Jason. What's the next act? Now do you tell me that it's healthy, that it's really good for me?"

"Why the compulsion to cheapen things, Lois?"

"How do you cheapen something already cheap?"

"I am not cheap!"

"Neither am I, dear. But we were capable of a cheap relationship."

He studied her. "What if I asked you to marry me?"

She looked startled for a moment, and then smiled. "You can't make it into something special that way. That's just an extension of the love rationalization. And, you know, you might even do it if I said yes, just to prove to yourself that you are right and I am wrong. What kind of a marriage would that be?"

He shook his head. "I give up."

"Please do."

"Lois, what kind of a relationship *will* you accept?"

She picked up a pencil and tapped her lips with it, holding her head on the side, looking at him with a rather cold amusement. "It would be sort of childish to say none at all, I guess. We started to be friends, but now we're not. But I did like being your friend. Maybe, if we were very very careful not to remind each other in any way of what happened Thursday night, we could get away from this sexual rivalry thing and get to be friends again."

"Do you think that if we do get to be friends, some time we can talk about it with . . . more understanding?"

"There's nothing more to say about it, Jason."

Her gray eyes looked into his, steadily, defiantly. The dark dress fit her figure beautifully, showing to advantage the slenderness of her waist, the firm round pressure of hips and thighs, the strong breasts. She looked brisk, tidy, immaculate and invulnerable. Already she was making it fade for him, making it difficult for him to believe that all of this warm fortress had crumpled and surrendered, gasping with urgen-

cies, making little broken cries as she sought total closeness, groaning his name.

In every truth, no matter how great or small, he thought,
there is a crumb of paradox, a small and dubious erosion.
And her life has somehow given her that kind of micro-vision
which focuses entirely on the doubt, denying the existence
of truth beyond her point of vision. So she can not ready
herself for love until she can see that all things are a mixture,
all things ambivalent, and life is a process of grasping the
entirety, satisfying yourself with a net balance for good. Hers
is the pitiful fate of untempered idealism which accepts nothing unless it is totally good—and because life does not strike
such bargains—ends by accepting nothing. Yet thinks herself
a cynic rather than an idealist. Senses her own waste of herself. Acted with sensual honesty, then feels shamed and
tries to shame me. Cheapness is in the people, not the deed.
Which, of course, is another kind of idealism, perhaps in its
own way as spurious as hers.

"Are you free for lunch?" he asked.

"Things have eased off a little now. Unless George comes
back and loads me up, yes."

For a moment she looked very vulnerable. "And don't try
to be clever with me, Jason. I'm not very clever. You know
that now. Just . . . be my friend."

Lunch was difficult. There was so much awareness, and she
wanted to bury it carefully under neat layers of polite talk,
patting each one down, smoothing the edges, restoring all
the strata to the way it was originally, so that eventually it
could be covered with sod so scrupulously fitted that one
could walk right on by it without knowing it was there. He
tried to help her, because the concealment seemed such a necessity to her. But from time to time the talk would veer toward an inadvertent innuendo, and then she would go on too
hastily, her voice a little thin.

It reminded him of something which had happened when he
had been five or six years old, and he wished he could tell
her about it, but he sensed she was in no mood to be
amused by it. A woman had come to visit his mother, and
he had never seen her before, but his mother had given him
strenuous warnings beforehand not, under any circumstances,
to stare at the woman or say anything or in any way show
any awareness of the fact that she had a truly monstrous nose,
a great fleshy appendage that dwarfed all the rest of her

face. After the first shocked glance, he had been very good about it. But that nose seemed to fill his consciousness. He tried to think of other things. But he marveled at the nose. His mother asked him to pass the little cakes, and he took the plate to the lady and avoided looking directly at her, and said, very politely, "Would you like another nose?"

There were the inadvertent innuendoes, and there was also the temptation to guide the conversation into areas where such allusions would be more frequent, keeping awareness alive without seeming to be trying to do so. But she was a subtle and clever woman, and he feared that if she guessed his intent, there would be no further chances to be near her. So he tried earnestly to do it her way. It was not easy. He had become so sensitized to her that he could be following what she was saying, and then notice a turn of her wrist or the shape of her mouth or the velvety look of the skin of her throat, and what she was saying would merge and blur into gibberish, and he would sit in a steamy and foolish agony, nodding, keeping the polite attentive look fixed on his face. It was easier for him when he kept talking, and he heard himself giving a learned lecture on why the eastern sections of most of the great cities of the world are the slum sections and why London was no exception and how the fifteen thousand bombs that fell onto the east end had given the planners and urban architects a rare chance to try to reverse the trend of hundreds of years.

George sat down with them and said, "If you're with this character, Lois, and a mosquito bites you, he'll tell you how they built the Panama Canal and whipped the yellow fever. Keep lecturing, pal."

"I'd finished that one, George."

"I got a little chore for you, Lois. Ida took the call. They missed the train. Now it's the six fifty-six."

"Call Aunty Beth?"

"Call that dear old lady," George said.

"It isn't going to be easy."

"I've got a few little problems too. And so has Ida. We had her set up for fittings, for rehearsal on a couple new things came in. We got New York phone calls piled up for her. What she needs now is run around in the cold with that kid and get a nice cold in the throat. That would fix the whole wagon. Suppose you go call that sweet old lady."

Lois hurried off. George ordered a bland lunch. Jason asked

for more coffee. George said, "How is it with you and Marney, pal?"

"We're friends."

George eyed him shrewdly. "That's nice. For a while there she was working a lot of little questions in, about you. But she stopped."

"Maybe she got all the answers she needs, George."

"Needs for what?"

"I wouldn't have the faintest idea."

"And what would you have in mind?"

"To be a friend, George."

"Everybody needs friends. Lois needs friends. Jenny needs friends."

"I approve of your wholesome philosophy, George."

"Lois was awful jumpy yesterday morning. And pale as a ghost."

"I'd guess it was a little hangover, wouldn't you?"

George studied him for a moment. "Okay. It's none of my business."

"What's none of your business?"

"End of conversation. New topic, Jase. Last night was a smash. Rave reviews. So far I can't find a bad one. Maybe the clipping service will find one, like in the *Manchester Guardian* or someplace, but it doesn't seem likely. What it was last night, it was love. Big waves of it rolling out of her into that audience and bouncing on back to her. They asked for all of it and got it, and I thought she wouldn't move a muscle until noon, but she was out early with the kid."

"What do you think of the boy?"

"I think he's trouble."

"Personally, not professionally, what do you think of him?"

George shrugged. "Seems like a nice enough kid. Something about a kid talking in that accent, it makes them all sound a little upstage and snotty. Like they were having you on. I believe like Paar does, you shake an Englishman awake in the middle of the night, he'd talk just like anybody."

"George, you are provincial."

George grinned. "I'm an international hick. Here she comes."

Lois slid into her chair. "That dear little old lady doesn't flutter at all. She gets veddy veddy icy. She said she had had quite enough of this nonsense."

"She's not alone," George said.

"She was very convincing. We had better get the boy on that train, George."

"I am going to make a special effort."

But Jenny did not return to the hotel with Matthew until half-past six. George, Lois, Jason and Ida were gathered in the sitting room of the suite, having a drink, trying to hide the growing tension when they heard Jenny and the boy coming down the corridor, singing some sort of school song.

They came into the suite, flushed and breathless and happy. The boy stopped singing the moment he saw the others in the room. They were arm in arm. The boy gently disengaged himself and pulled his cap off.

"We've been halfway up the Thames," Jenny said joyously.

"Down," the boy said.

"And all the way down the Strand."

"Up," the boy said.

"And we saw St. Paul's and the Tower Bridge and a gorgeous old clipper ship and the place where they measure time from."

"Greenwich Mean Time," the boy explained politely, and helped Jenny off with her coat.

"And when I was freezing he was perfectly comfortable because they take cold showers at that school." She sighed. "I don't know when I've had so much fun."

"And you missed the train," George said.

"On purpose," Jenny said blithely.

Matthew looked worried. "How did Aunty Beth take it, Miss Marney? I should have phoned her up myself, but . . ."

"She was upset," Lois said.

Ida spoke to Jenny. "You haven't much time. Shall I order dinner?"

"We ate," Jenny said.

"Twice," the boy said.

"You missed a few appointments here and there," George said sourly.

She faced him with a look of indignation. "Come off it, Georgie. I was very very good for days and days, and I followed your little schedules to the letter, and we're booked practically solid, aren't we, and good reviews?"

"Okay, okay," George said. "Come on, kid. We're going to have to scramble if I'm going to get you onto that train."

"Yes sir," Matthew said.

"*Just* a moment!" Jenny said. "Did you forget our surprise, dear?" she said to the boy. She turned to George. "I have persuaded Mr. Donne to be my guest for one more night and one more morning."

The boy bit his lip. "But, Jenny, we didn't *actually* . . ."

"But, darling, we did talk about that exhibit thing at the Science Museum."

"The ionic propulsion exhibit," the boy said dubiously.

"It would be *very* educational. Your Aunty Beth would certainly understand about that. And we haven't had a chance to get you that tape recorder you . . ."

"But Father promised to take me to buy one."

"I'd love to get one for you, Matthew. Really."

"I suppose he might not have a chance, really. . . ."

"And that exhibit would be educational, wouldn't it?"

"Oh yes, but . . ."

"Then it's settled. Come on, Lois. You call her and if it gets a little rough, you can turn her over to me, and I'll explain." They went into Jenny's bedroom and closed the door.

The boy looked worried. "I do seem to be taking up so much of her time."

"It seems to be what she wants, kid," George said wearily.

The boy smiled. "She seems to make rather a habit of getting what she wants."

"That's a good word for it," Jason said. "A habit."

The boy looked at his watch. "I've missed the train. We couldn't possibly make it now, Mr. Kogan."

Lois and Jenny came out of the bedroom. Jason saw that Lois wore a strained expression. Jenny said gayly, "It's perfectly all right with Aunty Beth."

"Really!" the boy said. He smiled broadly. "That's wizard."

"Tonight you can be backstage, if you'd like."

"Oh, I would like that very much, Jenny. I should go wash, if you would excuse me."

The boy went to his room. As soon as the door closed behind him, Lois said, "You know, Jenny, he's going to find out it isn't perfectly all right with Aunty Beth."

"What happened?" Jason asked.

"As soon as I told her what the plans were, she sniffed and hung up on me."

"It has to be all right with her, doesn't it?" Jenny said. "What can she do?"

George sighed. "I give up. All I ask, Jenny, don't parade the kid."

"I'm proud of him! I feel as if I want to wear him like a badge of honor."

"That isn't what the publicity would say."

"All right, George. I'll be careful. All day long, only three people recognized me, and they were very sweet."

George beckoned to Lois. "Come on, girl. We got chores."

As Lois left, she pointed out the clippings she had put on the coffee table. Jenny went over and began to look through them.

"I better be going along," Jason said.

"Don't go, Brownie. Ida has that look in her eye."

Ida folded her arms. "Why should I save it because he's here? He's thinking the same things I'm thinking. He's wondering the same things. So is George. We're none of us against you, Jenny B. We're all on your side."

"Sure," Jenny said. "Sure you are."

"I want to know one thing. How long is this going to go on?"

Jenny studied a clipping. "How long is what going to go on?"

"The Jenny Bowman Day Nursery."

Jenny put the clipping down carefully, straightened and gave Ida a long quiet look. "As long as I want."

Ida did not answer. Jenny looked appealingly at Jason. He merely looked at her.

"So I took him out for the day!" Jenny said with forced anger. "What's so wrong about that?"

"This is me. Ida. Remember? Eighteen years. And that fellow sitting over there is Jason Brown. Have either of us ever tried to do you any harm?"

"I just want to get to know him a little. That's all."

"And then what?" Ida asked.

Jenny moved across the room to where hatboxes were stacked. "Oh, they brought the hats," she said with forced animation. She took one out, turned to the mirror and tried it on.

"Let him go home, Jenny," Jason said.

"Tomorrow."

"Why don't you quit while you're ahead?" Ida asked.

Jenny did not answer. She continued to stare at herself in the mirror. Jason saw her reflection. Her eyes looked vast and her mouth trembled.

Ida went to her and put her arm around her. "Sure, you

just want to get to know him. With you, Jenny, it starts the same way and it ends the same way. You wanted to see him? Great. Fine. You saw him. *Now say good-by!* But you don't want that. You got to have a situation. Big feelings. And in the end, what are you going to have? Another pain in your heart. Why do you do it?"

Jenny gently turned out of Ida's clasp. She took off the hat and threw it aside. She looked expressionlessly at Ida. "I have to keep him with me as long as I possibly can. I have to. What else do you want to know?"

Ida bit her lip and turned away and went into her own room.

Jenny stood still for a moment, then fled blindly to Jason, piled herself into his lap and ground her face into his throat. "I hurt everybody," she whispered in her misery.

"We can get over it. We don't want you to hurt yourself."

"I hurt already, Brownie. I hurt bad. But not when my son is with me. Then it stops."

In one of her abrupt changes of mood she scrambled to her feet and grinned down at him. "Why are we all getting so sour, for God's sake? Life is a ball. We running a morgue around here? Rise and shine, Brownie. Are you good to my Lois? Be very good and sweet to her. She could be good for you. You know, Brownie, you've been settling into a rut. You know that, don't you? Getting more rumply and quiet and benign all the time. Sitting around watching life. You got to get into the middle of it and swing, dear. You can't sit it out. You and Lois can't sit it out. I built you up big."

"Thanks a lot."

"I didn't do anything wrong, did I?"

"No, Jenny. You couldn't possibly do anything wrong."

She stamped her foot. "Dammit, when I try to be a little bit happy, everybody else goes sour on me. What's wrong with everybody? Is this tour jinxed? Get out of here. Find Gabe and get him in here. My hair looks like a dog's bed."

That night, at the performance, Jason Brown—without plan or intent—caught himself and Lois Marney off guard. He was standing in the wings with Lois, watching Jenny on stage. The boy was nearby, his face rapt. George was standing with Ida. Jenny had begun her arrangement of "What Is This Thing Called Love." She began it with a slow, moody, quiet opening, with a pin spot on the guitarist who was the only accompaniment in the beginning. Later it would build and build as the band came in, section by section. But in the beginning it was very quiet, her voice and phrasing giving the worn lyrics a special intensity. He looked at Jenny and at the boy. He looked at Ida and George. He was aware of Lois beside him in the darkness. All of them were trapped in the spell Jenny was weaving, and the huge audience was as silent as though the theater were empty. He thought of the relationships of all of them to Jenny and to each other and he leaned toward Lois, and with a feeling of wryness, he whispered, "It's a very good question."

She gasped and turned toward him, her oval face a pallor in the shadows, and he knew he had read her mood without meaning to, and had startled her. For an instant she seemed warm and vulnerable in the darkness, seeming to sway toward him, and then she turned and was gone. He stood alone, pulling down the corners of his mouth. It was still an excellent question, one that Miss Marney might give some thought to. As the sections of the band began to come in, Jenny's voice expanded, and it took on that dark and smoky quality of the yearning and the despair she could put into that tired old song and make it new every time she did it.

After the show a score of old friends jammed the dressing room and corridor, good friends from all the years of the songs and the shows, the wildness and the heartbreaks, the raves and disasters. Hugs and kisses, and all the in-talk and the jokes and gossip, and the little edges of jealousy and need, padded and concealed by the cosmetic habit of gayety. Here was all the warmth of a special business, a special breed, and Jenny was totally responsive to it, funny, glittering, loving, spreading herself among all of them, merging it all into party and holiday, making of it, as she so often could, the best of all possible times for everyone.

Jason saw, beyond the tailored shoulders and the creamy bare ones, beyond the jewels and champagne glasses, the Donne boy in a corner, watchful and awed and uncomprehending, so he worked his way through the crush to Jenny and, when he had a chance, said to her that it looked as if it was shaping up into the kind of evening the boy might not enjoy.

She frowned at him. "But I want him with me!"

Jason indicated a couple of the more emotionally unstable

personalities of the industry. "To further his education?" he asked.

She pursed her lips. "Then we'll both go home."

"The kid is hungry and sleepy, and you'll want to rejoin the group as soon as he falls asleep."

She hesitated and then nodded and kissed his cheek. "Old Brownie, always taking good care."

She went and said good night to the boy and sent him back to the hotel with Lois. Jason wanted to go along with them, but at the time they left he could not conveniently disentangle himself from the attentions of a tiny redhead who had suddenly remembered a debt of gratitude. After she had been professionally dead for several years as a result of several nothings in a row, he had tailored a television script for her and battled the producer-director to get her cast in it, and she had done so well, so superbly well, that it had re-established her, complete with Emmy nomination and subsequent meaty roles in reasonably successful moving pictures. He knew she was well into her forties, but she was still an effective and magical twenty-eight, even at closest range—the result of a good five hours a day of working at it, plus the device of the sub-coiffure braids to pull her face firm in lieu of any telltale uplift incisions. So she pranced elfin and slightly stoned among the bigger folk, erect to enhance the pointy little breasts, agile to flaunt the perky little rump, batting the great sea-green eyes at him, telling him how truly and dearly and forever she loved and worshipped and adored darling Jason Brown, who was only just a little ol' writer, but had gotten her into just the right spot in spite of all the other people clamoring for her at the time. By the time she was momentarily distracted, the chance to leave with Lois was gone.

George Kogan made some skilled telephone calls, and the impromptu party moved to a private dining room in a famous restaurant, and picked up some more recruits. From there it fragmented slightly, but the nucleus moved on to the large flat of a suave, elderly, corseted British actor, and at something after two o'clock, the grateful tiny little redhead shucked her ex-husband escort and her agent-manager and went back to her borrowed apartment with Jason Brown, who, despite a certain vagueness induced by Scotch and champagne, was not at all convinced that this was one of his better ideas.

The interlude in the apartment quite cruelly confirmed his

uneasiness. Faced with the responsibility of such an intimate expression of gratitude, the tiny redhead was sobered by the fear that such intemperance might undo some of the benefits of the five dedicated hours per day. She was nervous about it, but convinced that she was affording this poor humble man one of the greatest moments of his life. She set the scene with the greatest care, adjusting the bedroom lighting, turbanning her hair in such a way it could not possibly become mussed, swathing her little breasts in a protective night-bra, and ensconcing herself in the big canopied bed like a fragile little bonbon in a lace candy box. Her nervous instructions covered not bruising her mouth, no pummeling, no crushing, no scratching or biting or anything like that of course, and don't take long.

Jason embraced her with due care, and listened to her sweet dutiful little manufactured sighs, and was suddenly and quite unfortunately reminded of a game of jackstraws, where the object was to remove one straw with such guile and delicacy the rest of the stack remained undisturbed. And with that image his last chance of consummation was lost. She offered false sympathy but no assistance. Her relief at being so unexpectedly freed of the obligation was complete and transparent. She donned a sheer little hip-length nightie that matched her eyes, sat joyously on the edge of the bed and gulped a glass of brandy so large it effectively removed any chance of cooperation in the immediate future. Moments after she finished it, she gave him a wide and glassy smile and toppled back into sleep, the empty glass bouncing and rolling across the thick carpeting. He slid her into the bed, covered her over, turned out the lights and let himself out. The ex-husband was waiting on the street. From ten feet away he snarled, drew his fist back and took three running steps at Jason and swung. Jason side-stepped and the man fell over a low hedge into a narrow area of grass. Jason looked over the hedge. The man lay on his back glaring up at him.

"That'll teach you not to mess with her!" the man said.

"It sure will," Jason said, and went off in search of a taxi. When he got to bed he could not go to sleep. It was after four in the morning. His male pride felt slightly damaged but there was an ironic amusement and a feeling of relief that far outweighed the small feeling of inadequacy. He wondered if the relief was due to a recognition of the absence of guilt that unfaithfulness to Lois would have caused. Yet the guilt, in any rational anaysis, should be as great as if he had accepted the gesture of gratitude. A weakness of the flesh should not cancel out the willingness of the spirit. But the spirit had not been very willing. It was more comforting to believe that it had been a reluctance of the spirit which had caused the weakness of the flesh.

Faithfulness to Lois was a rather frail theorem. It implied emotional dependence and obligation, which she stolidly refused to accept.

And at last he accepted the truth he was trying to avoid. He was a creature of staunchly middle-class morality, forever stuck with the concept that the gratifications of the body without emotional involvement are not only markedly grubby—they are even silly. And that tiny nervous woman, so convinced that she was making a gift beyond price, was the very stuff of comedy.

One day, he thought as he was sinking into sleep, he would tell Lois about it and they would laugh. The thought woke him up again. From whence came this confidence that he would ever be able to confide such things to Lois? She was a cripple. She had warmth, intelligence, humor, subtlety, but it all came to an abrupt stop at the lip of the chasm that flawed her—and beyond that point there was no humor, no warmth, no understanding at all. If she could ever be mended, she would be one of the rare ones, one of those who could fill your life from rim to rim and give every day a meaning beyond what words could express.

His only hope was his feeling that Lois was subjectively aware of that flaw, and though she did not dare admit it, wanted to be whole.

nine

JASON ARRIVED at the suite at twenty minutes before noon. The boy was sitting with the air of someone who has waited a long long time, and he got to his feet as Jason came in. He was alone.

"Good morning, sir."

"Good morning, Matt. What's the word on Jenny?"

The boy sat down again. His smile was slightly wan. "Miss Ida says she's out. That's French, she says, for not up yet."

"Last night got a little congested."

"She does have a great many friends, doesn't she?"

Jason sat on the couch. "Some of them are Jenny's friends. And a lot of them are friends of Jenny Bowman."

"I see what you mean, sir. I suspect I might be both." There was a glint of solemn humor in his dark eyes. Jenny's eyes, Jason thought.

"Nobody could blame you for that."

"I recognized so many of them, Mr. Brown. You know, they all seem rather smaller than I imagined, smaller people physically."

"The camera tends to inflate everything, Matt. I guess you've had a dull morning."

"I don't mind, really. I shall have another chance. But I thought she might find it interesting. Perhaps, with the way she works, sleep is more important for her. Earlier this morning, Mr. Kogan said Miss Marney might go with me, but I thought Jenny might wake up at any time . . ." The boy frowned. "Of course, I have missed another train by now. I seem to have missed a great many trains lately."

"How did you like being backstage?"

"Most interesting. It wasn't as I imagined. I rather expected everyone would be . . . matter of fact. But everyone seemed so excited and happy, even the ones who do things with the lights and curtains."

"It's like that when she works. It might not be the same with other performers."

"She's really very special, isn't she?"

"There's only one."

"I imagine she makes a great deal of money at it." The boy flushed. "I'm sorry. That was a rude thing to say."

"Not at all, Matt. She doesn't really make very much. The tour is set up so that she gets a guarantee and a percentage of the house over that guarantee. All the payroll and tour expenses, transportation, music, musicians and so on come out of that. What's left over goes to her agent. He takes his percentage and sends what's left to her financial manager. He also gets the income from her records, movie contracts and so on. He pays the bills, sets money aside for taxes, makes investments if there is any left over to invest, and deposits her allowance in her personal account. If the whole tour is booked absolutely solid and they don't run into any unexpected expenses, there may be three or four thousand dollars left over for investment at the end of it. But while the tour is going on, she is living first class, traveling first class. If she should break even, the tour does indirectly improve record sales and movie box office. She could cut the payroll way down and make a lot more by taking extended club dates. But this tour thing is part of her image. It is what Jenny Bowman does. Do you understand that?"

"I think so, sir. Thank you for . . . telling me so much that isn't any of my business, I suppose. It really is quite chancy then."

"Very chancy. She enriches theater owners and producers and record companies, and, with the way the taxes go, she gets the short end of the stick. And she's been fattening a lot of people for a lot of years. So they call her a property, and they use every pressure in the world to keep her working."

"But she does seem to enjoy it, Mr. Brown."

"It might be more necessary to her than she would like to think."

"I don't know quite what you mean, sir."

Ida came in through the corridor door and the tiny foyer. She said good morning and looked inquisitively at Matthew Donne. He shook his head. "Not much of a morning for ionic propulsion," she said. "I'll take another look."

She went into Jenny's bedroom. She came out in a few moment and said, "There are some signs of life in there, boy. Why don't you go on in and thump around a little? If it bites, we've got some iodine."

"Is it really all right?" the boy asked.

"Go ahead."

The boy went in, and left the door ajar. In a little while they heard the boy's polite voice, Jenny's slumbrous murmurs—with a note of apology.

"Thick as thieves," Ida murmured.

"Any response from Aunty?"

"A deadly silence."

The boy came out of the bedroom and closed the door. "She's going to get dressed now, Miss Ida."

"Before breakfast?"

"We are to have something called a brunch, I believe. And do some shopping. She . . . she is very sorry about the ionic propulsion."

"Shopping on Sunday?" Ida asked.

The boy looked startled. "So it is: I seem to be losing track."

"You're not alone," Ida said mildly.

Jason Brown found Lois having lunch alone. She welcomed him with an animation and a warmth which astonished him. She had just begun, and asked him to join her.

"I've been wondering about my guide to local scenes and wonders," she said. "If you haven't any other plans." She wore a burgundy-red suit, a gray silk scarf at her throat, a hat that suited her well.

"If George hasn't any other plans for you?"

"He can't possibly get back here before one thirty, and it will probably be two o'clock, and if we have any sense we'll be gone by then."

"So we'll be gone by then."

After he had ordered, she smiled mockingly at him. "You look a little eroded, my friend."

"It was one of those evenings where you never finish a sentence, and you never hear anybody else finish one either."

She made a face. "I hate those."

"Occupational hazard."

"Thank God I got out of it."

"I tried to leave with you, but you took off too fast, Lois. And there was another disappointed fellow too."

"Who? Oh, the narrow little Frenchman in the elevator shoes. He kept staring at me. Like Hillary looking at Everest."

"By the time he went and got his crampons, his oxygen equipment and his ice axe, you were gone. He wept bitterly."

"I had a much better time with Matthew. Better than I expected, really. He thinks he might become an anthropologist. This is his first experience living with the aborigines. The tribal customs fascinate him. Real live Americans. He thinks we're a little more complex and difficult than we're reported."

"He can do a paper on us."

"Where are we going, Jason?"

"It's a cold bright day with no wind. So we'll do the excusion boat thing, and then if you have time we'll go to the Tate."

"If I brought my little camera would you pretend you didn't know me?"

"I'll use it for you. I'll pose you in front of national monuments."

"Smirking."

"Having wonderful time. Wish you were here. Regards to the gang."

"I have to be back at six. So does Jenny. Cocktails for the ladies of the press."

"I thought they'd covered them all."

"The weighty ones. This is the rabble. Fashion people and food people and lovelorn advice people and so on."

"By the time you get your coat and camera, I'll be waiting in the lobby."

When Jason and Lois returned to the hotel at ten minutes to six, George Kogan descended on them when they were a dozen feet inside the lobby. He was scowling, jittery and angry. "Where the hell is she?" he demanded.

Lois stared at him calmly. "First you say hello. And then we say hello. And then you ask me if I had a good time. Yes, I did, thank you. And neither of us have the slightest idea where Jenny is. I thought she'd be back by now."

"So did I."

"Did you remind her of this?" Jason asked.

"Seven times. And so did Ida. And Ida reminded her again when she phoned in and said the boy is staying over tonight too. Do you want to phone Canterbury again, Lois?"

"I don't think so."

"I didn't think you would. I got that room on the mezzanine floor. All those women are up there, knocking off the cocktails, gobbling up the canapes, telling each other what they're going to ask Jenny. What am I supposed to do? She promised she'd be back. She's out of her so-called mind. I better get up there. Lois honey, you stay right here and the minute she comes in, *if* she comes in, shoo her up to that room and send the boy up to the suite. Okay?"

"Yes sir, George, sir."

"And I'll see if I . . ." He stopped suddenly and looked speculatively at Jason. Still staring at Jason, he relit his chewed cigar. "You can take a little pressure off me, old pal."

"Now *wait* a minute!"

"You're going to be a substitute celebrity, pal."

"But, George, I'm only a . . ."

"You're somebody who's willing to ask me for a lot of favors. Right?"

Jason looked helplessly at Lois. "You're hooked, dear," she said cheerfully. "Just do what they all do. Make up interesting answers."

George took him up the stairs to the mezzanine. At the top of the stairs Jason looked back forlornly at Lois. She beamed and threw him a kiss. As they walked toward the door of the room where the conference was to take place, Jason cringed at the babble of female voices, the sounds of high-pitched laughter.

George paused and squared his shoulders and went in. The room seemed full of women. They were around the canape table. Waiters were passing the cocktail trays. The sounds faded and all the expectant eyes stared at the two of them.

George smiled at them and waved his cigar. "Girls— Jenny's asked me to stand in for her today. She loves to talk to the Ladies of the Press and she's very disappointed not to be here. But please eat, have fun—and if you have any questions, think of me as though I were Jenny."

"When did you start smoking cigars?" one of them asked. There was mild laughter, and too much hearty laughter from George. Jason smiled wanly.

"Just where is Miss Bowman?" another one asked.

"There's a chance, just a chance, mind you, she might still make it," George said. "But it doesn't look good. Frankly, it's one of those purely legal and technical things. A business meeting. No interest to you ladies at all. And it's gone on way beyond time. Way, way beyond."

"Who designed the costume she wore last night?" someone asked.

"Before we get into the questions, ladies, I've got a surprise for you. You will certainly want to ask him some questions. I'm proud to present Mr. Jason Brown, the famous playwright from Hollywood, California. Mr. Brown flew in last week and he's working with Jenny on the script of the picture she's going to do when this six-country tour is ended. It's called *The Longest Dawn* and it is going to be one of the greatest pictures of all time, and it will star Jenny Bowman. Mr. Brown has consented to answer any questions you wish to ask him about Hollywood and the stars and his writing career."

The little gasps and coos of pleasure astonished Jason Brown. But he could see a few faces registering that total indifference he had expected from all of them.

"Now the way we'll do this," George said, "as soon as Mr. Brown and I get a drink in hand, we'll take opposite ends of this room and you girls just move right in on us with your questions."

Jason acquired a martini and got into position with his back to the wall. A dozen of them hemmed him in. Almost that many surrounded George. Some of them moved from group to group. At first too many of them tried to ask questions at once. But soon it became reasonably well-organized. Some of the questions were asinine. Some of them were all too shrewd. Many of them were about Jenny. Little by little they acquired information about him. Jason had the feeling that he was like a large artichoke being devoured by a hungry mob. They pulled off leaf after leaf, removing his outer covering, working their way down to the surprisingly small amount of nourishment within.

After an hour the pressure dropped. They began to excuse themselves and leave. By that time he had become aware of one woman who asked no questions at all. Sometimes when he looked into the middle distance to organize his answer, he would catch her eye and she would stare at him with a mocking expression. She looked quite unwholesome. He thought she could have been reasonably attractive if she made any effort. She had a ripe figure, a rather fleshy face, a cold pale blue eye, a snaggle of dark blonde hair, a broad and careless smear of lipstick. She wore a blue dress that seemed too small for her, and a ratty fur cape. It was almost excessively obvious that she wore nothing under the blue dress. It looked as though she had slept in it. The other women seemed to avoid looking at her or speaking to her. She merely stood and ate vast quantities of the canapes and smoked many cigarettes in a long white holder and looked bored, indifferent and savagely amused.

George took his first chance and left quickly, with a parting wave toward Jason. There were six around Jason and then three and then two. The two left together, after effusive thanks, slightly tight, full of misinformation. And then he was alone in the room with the woman in the blue dress. Service people came in to clean up the debris. ·

"If you have no questions . . ."

"Oh, but I do!" she said, and popped a last canape into her mouth and delicately wiped her fingers on the fur of her cape. She moved closer to him and smiled impudently at him. "You could take me down and buy me a proper drink," she said. "I hate and despise this cocktail slop." He detected her abundant use of a very heavy musky perfume.

"I wish I could, but . . ."

"Oh, surely you can, Jason. A very old and very dear friend of mine said you would talk to me nicely, should the chance arise. And I'd much rather talk to you than to Kogan. After all, you were *much* closer to Jenny once upon a time." Her manner of speech was a curious mixture of affectation and cockney.

"An old friend?" he asked blankly.

"Yes. He told me to stay close to the Bowman party. And keep in touch with him. He even gave me some funds for expense money, before he left. You might even say he started me in this business. Sam Dean. You *will* buy me that drink?"

"It will be my pleasure, Miss . . ."

"Landor. Beth Landor."

"What paper are you with?"

"Not with any of them. And then again with all of them, you might say. I free-lance a bit. When one comes up with something interesting, it's rather an advantage to be able to trade about, I find. I do have press credentials, of course. Otherwise I couldn't have come to this little fete."

"I would like to see if George Kogan could join us, Miss Landor."

She hooked her arm around his and smiled up at him. "I think we should keep this quite private, Jason. At least for now."

At a table in a dark corner of the lounge, she ordered a

double Scotch on ice and a package of cigarettes. She smiled cozily at him and said, "This is better for a private talk, isn't it? All those gabbing women! My word! I suppose we should get right to it. Who is the young lad, Jason?"

"Young lad?"

She laughed. "You actually look ill! It must be something quite sticky. And I suppose you would keep on fencing indefinitely, wouldn't you? My dear fellow, Sam Dean wouldn't entrust anything to anyone without resource, would he? I shall tell you *some* of the things I know. Not all, because if you are not certain how much I know, it should keep you from lying. The boy's name is Matthew Donne. His father is a widower, Mr. David Donne, a Wimpole Street surgeon. The boy is on vacation from Canterbury School. But we get back to my question, do we not? Who is the lad? Why does she give him so much time? Why does she skulk out of the hotel with him?"

Jason hoped and prayed his imitation of ease was convincing. The woman sipped her drink. She had a sensuous and bovine look, as though she would be more at home working as a stripper in one of the little Soho theater clubs, or bumping and grinding her way across the stage of the venerable Windmill Theatre. But the clear cold intelligence in those pale blue eyes was unsettling.

He experimented with a mild laugh and hoped he brought it off. "She skulks as you call it, to get a little privacy I suppose. Donne has treated her for throat problems. That's his specialty. He and Jenny are friends. The doctor was called away on an emergency case. This is the boy's vacation time, and the doctor had promised him a few days in London, so Jenny is filling in. She likes the boy. He's a pretty good boy. I don't think there's much mystery about it, Miss Landor."

"I just wouldn't say Jenny Bowman was the sort to waste her time on children. It seems odd."

"I guess it's sort of an obligation to see that the boy has a good time."

"Could you cry out for another of these, please? You know, Jason, what Sam Dean and I have is an instinct. When he fastened me onto this, I rather thought she might be on the tiles with someone unsuitable, you know? But it is something quite different, isn't it?"

He smiled. "Nice try, but I would say it's nothing at all."

"The doctor is a widower, of course."

"I wouldn't say they're friendly in that way, Miss Landor."

"Possibly she wants to expand the area of friendship. I understand the doctor is quite a handsome man. And successful. It would be a reason for being very nice to the boy, wouldn't it?"

At that moment Jason saw Lois come into the lounge. She stopped just beyond the door and looked around. She saw him and started toward the corner, hesitated, stopped, turned on her heel and went back out.

"Rather nice, that," Beth Landor said. "Did you keep her the night at The Draycott? It's a dreary place, actually. I've never understood why Tommy Bird seems so fond of it."

"We had supper there," he said.

"My word, you're actually offended, aren't you? No harm intended, Jason. She seems a hearty piece, and I was just curious. It's my disease, of course. Being curious."

"And you brought it up to prove how good you are at finding out things."

"Perhaps. It isn't much of a trick, you know. Doormen, switchboard people, taxi people, stagehands and so on. Once one learns how to use them properly, it's all quite simple."

"What do you want, Miss Landor?"

She tilted her head to one side and peered at him. "I'm not making it obvious? I want something dreadfully juicy and salable about your dear Jenny. It's presold to Sam Dean, naturally. But I can do rather well with it on the local front, you know."

"If I did know anything, and I assure you there is nothing, why in the world would I tell you?"

"Are you certain you haven't told me quite a bit, sweets? Perhaps you've simplified my little research chores. Here, dear. A little card with my number. My little studio apartment in Notting Hill. When I'm not there, there's a little box that takes messages."

"Why should I want to call you?"

She looked at him, and her heavy lip curled and lifted in an expression of delicate and unmistakable lust. "You might care to drop by for a little drink one evening, sweets." She gulped the rest of her second drink, smiled and stood up and slowly walked out of the lounge, her big soft hips flexing and clenching under the taut blue fabric of the wrinkled dress.

Jason hurried upstairs. They were all gone. He slipped a

scrawled note under George's door saying it was important they get in touch immediately. He went back down to the lobby and phoned Tommy Bird's home number.

"How'd you like the club?" Tommy asked as soon as he recognized the voice.

"It was very very good. And thank you for setting it up. But I should have been able to pay."

"Hell, we got room for it on the account, Jase," Tommy said. "I thought you'd like it. They know how to treat you. Want I should phone them again for you?"

"No thanks. What I called about, what do you know about a woman named Beth Landor?"

"I know she's bad news. Her stuff gets into the worst sheets they got in this town. And they've got some beauts. She is a very smart slob, and if she gets hold of anything, she can kill you. She works alone and then peddles it for the high bid."

"Tommy, what if the person she wants to write about comes up with the high bid?"

"No. I had to try that once. I went to the top offer I was authorized to give, and she just laughed at me. She likes to see her name in the paper. She likes to drop the bomb on people. Jase, is she onto something about Jenny?"

"She might be. I don't know. Just say she's getting close."

"Would it be bad?"

"Very very bad."

He heard Tommy Bird sigh. "All I can tell you, you better cover up as good as you can, and pray."

"I was afraid of that."

"If there was any way to get to her, I would have found it the time I was trying to buy her off."

"Well, we'll do what we can."

"Jase, you want to join us? We're going to Rule's for kidney pie. We'll be there in maybe forty minutes."

"Some other time, maybe. Thanks."

ten

JASON BROWN WAS NOT able to talk to George Kogan until after ten o'clock on Monday morning. He talked in George's room. George seemed distracted at first, but Jason soon had his full attention.

"That one in the blue dress? The big eater? The one with a head like an old mop?"

"That one. Yes."

George sat on his bed. "Sam Dean," he murmured. "Jesus! I guess we didn't do as good as we thought we did." He hit his thigh with his fist. "That settles it, pal. We've *got* to send that kid back where he belongs." He thought for a moment. Suddenly he looked up at Jason with a wry smile. "You bugged Marney, pal. She figured you'd made a new friend. She'll be glad to know you were in there fighting for the team."

"If she thinks I was attracted to that monster . . ."

"Let's go down the hall and bring her up to date."

Before going down the corridor, George checked the suite. Jenny was awake. She and the boy were having breakfast in her room, and planning their day. George told Ida not to let her leave before he saw her.

As they went down the corridor George said bitterly, "He didn't leave last night. He couldn't leave last night. Not when they got to go buy him a tape recorder. Nobody phones Aunty. Maybe Aunty shows up with some cops."

Lois called to them to come in. She was adding a column of figures. She gave Jason a frosty glance and a courteous good morning.

George straddled a straight chair and rested his arms on the back of it and grinned at Lois. "I want to set your mind at rest about the newspaper broad your friend Jason picked up."

She looked politely astonished. "Set my mind at rest? Did I seem uneasy about anything?"

"She's sort of working for Sam Dean. That's the name she

used to get Jase's attention. She specializes in scandal, honey.
And she wants to know why Jenny is spending so much time
on the kid."

Lois put her pen down and stared at them. "Really?"

"We were going to have dinner," Jason said, "but you disappeared."

She blushed. "I thought you seemed busy."

"He was very busy and he did pretty good," George said.
"And now you got him sore at you for you thinking he'd latch
onto a pig like that one."

"I didn't examine her very closely," Lois said. She blushed
again. "Why should I care what . . ."

"Okay," George said. "You don't care. But we've got us
a problem. So what you do, just in case, Lois, you get us a
piece of the receipts in cash, and we'll hold it handy in the
hotel safe."

"But Tommy said she won't . . ."

"This could be the first time," George said.

"How much?" Lois asked.

"Let's go for two thousand pounds."

"Blackmail money?" Lois said unhappily.

"The practical approach," George said. "Be ready for anything. Come on, Jase, let's go tackle our star."

Jason hung back for a moment. "I wasn't sore at anything," he said.

She nodded. "George imagines a lot of things. About . . .
everybody. I did have a wonderful time yesterday. Thank
you."

"Are you coming?" George called.

The boy had gone to his own room. Jenny came scurrying
out into the sitting room, smiling and happy. Ida was not
there. "Make it fast, men," she said. "We're off to . . ." She
stopped suddenly and looked intently at each of them.
"What's wrong?"

Jason started the story. She sat down and listened quietly.
George took over and finished it. "So you see," he said,
"the boy has to go."

"*Has* to go? I don't see that at all. Why shouldn't what
Brownie told her satisfy her?"

"We can't take that chance," George said.

"Suppose I'm willing to take that chance?"

George sat beside her and took her hand. "Jenny darling,
I've got to say some rough words to you. I hate to do it."

"You scare awful easy, George."

"You keep the boy around and that Landor woman is going to keep right on checking it out, and sooner or later she'll get the jackpot idea and then she'll find out just how old the boy is, add nine months to the age and find out just where you were and where the doctor was at that time. She's got Sam to help her on the other end. It won't be hard. It won't be hard at all."

"So?"

"Please, Jenny. Remember the deal with the Swede? The Stromboli thing?"

"Who doesn't?"

"You know what messed her up most? Not leaving her husband. It was the business of deserting her daughter. The kid was ten years old. The public couldn't forgive that, honey. Not for seven long years, not until the Italian left her and that made her an underdog again. Can't you see what would happen to you if it came out you'd given away the only baby you ever had? Can't you predict what they'd do to you? They'd tear you to ribbons and stomp you into the ground."

"George, do you really think that means very much to me right now?"

"It should, baby. It should."

The boy came into the sitting room, ready to go out. He greeted the two men. And then he became aware of the odd silence of Jenny. She was looking fixedly at George, tears caught in her lashes.

"I say, is anything wrong?" the boy asked anxiously.

Without taking her glance away from George, she said, "Matthew, do you remember what we talked about yesterday in that churchyard at Stoke Poges?"

"Yes, Jenny. Of course."

"You know I'm leaving for Paris in a few days, and I would very much like to have you come and spend the rest of your holiday with me. I'll talk to your father and I'll arrange everything. All you have to do is say yes."

The boy frowned. "But perhaps Mr. Kogan and Mr. Brown would rather I . . ."

"Come here, Matthew, please." She took his hand and looked at him. "I am inviting you. That's the only thing that matters."

"Jenny, I don't understand. Why are you being so kind to me?"

"Because I never had a son, and I'd like to pretend for a little while I have one. Will you help me pretend?"

The boy hesitated and then gave her a slow sweet smile. "Yes, Jenny."

She smiled back, gave him a quick hug and said, "Wait for me in the lobby, dear. I'll be along soon."

After the door closed behind the boy, George said, "Jenny, Jenny. What are you trying to prove?"

"I love my son," she said in a small voice.

"Do you know what you could be doing to him?"

"I want him near me. His father is coming back today."

"How do you know?"

"We called Miss Plimpton this morning. He'll be in on an afternoon flight."

George jumped up and waved his arms wildly. "Why ask the kid's father? Why bother with that? Hell, let's put the kid in a wardrobe trunk and smuggle him to Paris."

"Shut up, George. I'll need the car at two to go to the airport. I'll go alone. I'll leave Matthew here. I'll *make* David agree."

At four o'clock that afternoon, George came to Lois's room to get Jason. George looked subdued and worried. "She wants to cry on your shoulder, pal," George said. "The roof fell in and then the walls fell on top of the roof. Whether she goes on tonight is anybody's guess."

"Was it bad?" Jason asked.

"It was very very bad," George said.

Jason went down to the suite. Ida motioned toward the closed door of Jenny's bedroom. "Go right on in," she said in that tone usually reserved for times of mourning.

The draperies were drawn. She lay curled on the bed in the darkened room, her back toward the door. She wore the quilted yellow robe again, and she looked small and defeated. She turned and looked at him. "Oh, Brownie," she said in a heartbreak voice. "Brownie."

He went to her and sat on the bed. He patted her shoulder. "You run into stone walls," he said, "and pick yourself up and run into them again."

"I know. Brownie, it was awful. You have no idea."

And she told him about it, and made him see and feel exactly how it was. She'd had the driver take her to the airport. She waited for David Donne outside customs. When he had seen her, he had seemed slightly startled, but he had not smiled. He was grim and silent, and his mouth was hard. She told him about phoning Miss Plimpton and finding out about the flight. She told him she wanted to talk to him, and asked him to come along with her in the limousine. He said he had his own car and driver. "I'm on my way to the hospital," he said. "If you want to talk, you'd better come along with me." She dismissed her driver and went along with him.

She said the silence was awkward. She tried to make small talk about his trip to Rome. He was unresponsive. At last she said, "I have a confession to make."

"Have you?"

"I'm afraid I've done something I shouldn't have."

"I know," he said.

"How could you know?" she asked, shocked.

"His aunt called me, of course. What else could she do?"

"Are you terribly angry?"

"I'm so sick with anger I can hardly speak," he said in a quiet voice.

"I . . . I don't know what to say. Except that it's so wonderful being with him."

"There's just one thing I want to know. Did you tell him anything?"

"I swear I haven't."

"Are you quite sure? It isn't like the boy to be so reckless and thoughtless and inconsiderate."

"I've told him nothing. I guess you can be angry. But I haven't done him any harm."

"That remains to be seen."

"If I'm such an unsavory character, why did you let me see him in the first place, David?"

He glared at her. "Why did I . . . ?" He brought his temper under control. "As I remember, you did a great deal of begging and pleading."

"I never beg. . . ."

He stared at her, his face rigid. "No. You never beg. You just damned well *assume*. What you want, you just get. You were that way thirteen years ago and you haven't changed and you never will. You're nothing but a self-centered, grasping, little bitch!"

She felt the tears come into her eyes. "Is that what you think of me? How strange, I didn't think that . . ."

"Come off it, Jenny. It won't work this time. Your meeting me doesn't make me less sick at heart. I'll go to Canterbury this evening and have it out with the boy."

"To Canterbury?" she said, baffled.

His eyes widened. "Do you mean to say he is *still* with you?"

"Yes. The reason I came to see you at the airport, David, I want your permission to take him along to Paris for my opening there. After all, he is still on holiday and . . ."

He stared at her and slowly shook his head and told her she was an incredible person. He directed his chauffeur to the hotel. The remainder of the trip was silent. Before they entered the suite, Jenny stopped him and said, "Before you go in and play heavy father, remember that this was not his fault. This is all something I brought about. Keep that in mind, David."

When she opened the door he pushed by her, calling, "Matt? Matt?"

The boy came out of his room. Jenny said quickly, "Matthew, dear, we didn't win."

"Hello, father," the boy said uneasily. "I wanted to come along to the airport with Jenny, but she thought it better she talk to you alone about Paris and all."

"She explained it perfectly. All I want you to do now is pack up and come along. Are you ready?"

"No. But . . . there isn't much. It won't take me a minute."

"Hurry along, then. The car's outside."

"All right," the boy said and went into his room and closed the door.

"Paris," David said in a disgusted voice. "And Rome and Brussels and Berlin, the whole tour. Then maybe you could get him into the moving pictures."

"Oh for God's sake don't sulk. I'll say I'm sorry. Matthew will say he's sorry too. What do you want us to do? Grovel and sob?"

He stared at her. "I don't want you to do anything. I just want to get out of here as soon as possible."

She stared at him. "Just what was so terrible about having fun together? What's so shameful about that? Why should that give you the right to stand there and look at me as if I were a criminal?"

"You know what you did."

"All right. I broke a promise. I know it. All the years your wife was alive I kept out of the way, didn't I?"

"She was good for him."

"Fine! She was good for him. Congratulations! But what has he got now? You with your sour face, too busy to go visit him. And Aunty Beth who's about forty years too late. What kind of life is that for him?"

"You are either too stupid to realize, or to stubborn to admit that Matthew and I have a good relationship. We did very well before you came and we'll do very well after you leave."

"My God, you know how to strike a nerve, don't you? He needs me and I want him!"

"He's not yours to have, Jenny. You gave him to me a long time ago. I love him and I need him."

"*You* need *him*? He's a child, David. What does *he* need?"

"He's my son and I'm going to keep him!"

There was a heavy silence. Jenny turned toward David and said clearly, "There's just one little thing we may be overlooking, you know. He's my son too. I made him. So where do we go from there?"

Jenny began to cry as she told Jason about it. She turned her agonized face toward him. "Oh, Brownie. It was so awful."

"What happened?"

"Matthew. Matthew was . . . he was there, in the doorway. David saw him first. I don't know how long he'd been there. But you could see by his face that he'd heard it. He stood with his suitcase and that tape recorder, and he looked so white and sick. Neither of us could think of anything at all to say to him. He swallowed hard and came into the room and said he was all packed. His voice shook. He took his things over near the door and stood with his back to us after he put them down, and asked if . . . if it was true." She snuffled and blew her nose. "So David told him it was true. Then Matthew asked his father why he hadn't told him. David said he meant to, intended to, but he kept putting it off. Then he asked me why I hadn't told him. He looked so white and wretched and accusing. I said I'd promised his father not to. Then David decided it was time to leave. The boy didn't want to leave. He wanted to stay and get it all clearer in his mind. I had no objections. I said so. But then David reminded the boy how few orders, direct orders, he had ever given him. And he ordered him to leave. And Matthew, with a sort of shy and wonderful dignity turned to me and explained that he was leaving not because he wanted to, but because he had been ordered to. He asked me if he could phone me tomorrow and talk. I said I would like to have him do that. And then, as David was looking more and more surly, Matthew turned to him and said that he didn't expect he would be ordered not to phone his friends. It was very brave and very firm. And . . . and then they left. Oh, hold me, Brownie. Hold me close. I feel as if I was falling off the edge of the world."

He held her until the tears were under control.

"What shall I do?" she asked. "It isn't fair. It just isn't fair."

"I don't see that there's anything you can do, Jenny. You have no legal claim on the boy."

"No legal claim," she said thoughtfully.

"Now that the boy knows, he might insist on being permitted to see you once in a while."

"After David poisons his mind against me? No, I keep wondering if that is true, Brownie."

"If what is true?"

"That I have no legal claim at all. I wonder . . ."

"Jenny?"

"You have been a darling, Brownie. I love you. Now run along and send George in here. Find him and send him in here."

Jason heard the rest of it in the dressing room at the theater. George had briefed him on some of it. At Jenny's insistence he had made two long phone calls to the New York lawyers who had handled the adoption procedures. When Jenny came sweeping into the dressing room, she was holding her head high. She looked vibrant, narrow-eyed and dangerous. Her small jaw had a clamped and stubborn look. Ida was getting her costume ready. Gabe was ready to fix her hair.

George followed her in, practically wringing his hands. "Yes, darling, there is a case," he said.

"I told you, didn't I?" she said firmly. "Brownie, Ida, I've got a son."

"Did I say how much of a case?" George said. "What you got, Jenny, is a technicality. I've been telling you. The adoption was legitimate. But there's some kind of second papers or final papers. And you never signed them."

"Good for me!" she said pertly.

"Can't you slow down a little?" George demanded. "New York was very cold about this. You know? Frankly, it's a long shot. No guarantees. Nothing easy. A whole long Megillah in court. It would be a hell of a thing to fight."

"I'm a fighter, George, and I know what I'm fighting for. Tell them to go ahead and get it rolling."

"So you have to have lawyers here too."

"So they can pick some lawyers here. Tell them to get going."

George sighed heavily. "Gabe, Ida, Jase. Go take a coffee break or something."

"Better be a fast one," Ida said.

"Brownie stays," Jenny said. The other two left.

She was at the dressing table, sitting on the bench. George went up behind her and put his hands on her shoulders. "Leave out the lawyers one minute, Jenny. For advice take a little from me. Right now you are at the top of a career you've been building for twenty years. For half that time I've been with you, helping. Right?"

"Right," she said.

"So I know a little about the subject? And now that you've got the career neat and tight in your hot little hands I can't stand by and watch you toss it over the wall. . . . But more than that I can't stand by and see you destroy yourself."

"How?"

"So you fight the case. You may win. It's possible. I don't know. But do you know what it would mean? You'd have to stay right here in England and fight this thing out. You couldn't be in Rome one week and Miami the next. You'd have to be here in the courts. And that can be pretty rough. On you *and* the kid. The boy has a father, a home, a school, a way of life he knows. So you want to jump into the middle of that and make all kinds of waves."

"Yes. That's what I want."

"So you get him and what do you do with him. Trail all over the world dragging a tutor along? Hotel suites, rented cars, other people's houses. They're pretty tough in England about schooling. The court would have to decide that kind of life would be okay for him. They might say you'd have to leave him in school and see him now and then at vacation. Is that what you want? Don't you see?"

"Go on," she said and got up and went into the screened dressing area.

"And what would happen to you? How would you be able to work with this pull all the time? Do you know how to raise a boy? I'd say he's been raised fine so far. It's not all kisses and presents and supper after the show. It's a full-time

job, and dear, forgive me, but I don't think you know how
to do it. This is your job, right here, and you do it better
than anyone else in the world. You *know* it. Don't force this.
Let it rest. Don't give the whole world a fat chance to crucify
you for something that happened a long time ago. You bring
it out in the open, in the courts, and they'll make it stinking
dirty rotten for everybody. You want the lawyers on the
other side trying to prove you're not fit to have him? Let it
rest, darling. The kid is happy; he belongs. Leave him there.
Any other way may destroy you. And destroy your son too."

There was a long silence. Jenny came back out into the
dressing room wearing her costume. She smiled at George.
"You're terribly sweet, George, and I know you're trying to
help, but when you're lucky enough to find something that
really matters, the way I have, you have to hang onto it. I
love him, George. And do you know the strangest thing? I
think he loves me."

Ida knocked at the door and opened it. "We better come
in and get you set."

"Come on, then," George said hollowly.

"George?"

"Yes, Jenny."

"Just for luck, buy Matthew a ticket."

"To Paris?"

"No. For the whole tour."

"For the whole tour," George said emptily. He nodded. He
walked out of the dressing room. Ida and Gabe were working
on Jenny.

"George is right," Jason said.

"Is he? What things have the most meaning, Brownie?"

"The things you want the most, I guess."

"Exactly."

Jenny looked at Ida. "Please, Ida. Be happy for me. Don't
be angry. Don't think I'm crazy. And don't feel sorry for me.
Be happy and wish me luck."

Ida looked at her for a long moment. "Okay, Jenny B.
Luck."

The overture had started. Jenny listened, kissed Ida lightly
on the cheek, and then headed slowly for her place in the
wings.

eleven

JASON BROWN AWOKE Tuesday to a feeling of gray and sour depression. He could not remember his dreams, knew only that he had dreamed, had somewhere run and somewhere wept, but knew not why. He felt a half-step removed from reality, exiled in a cold place, charged with insoluble problems. He yearned for home sunshine, the cluttered workroom, Bonny's flower face. Here was only the cold wet springtime, and Jenny Bowman plunging into a destruction no one could halt. Here was Lois, denying the abundant gifts of her warmth, rejecting herself and trying to think it wisdom. Here, in a strange city, where his memories of Jocelyn and Joyce were bittersweet, he would now be privileged to watch the end of something else. He got up feeling seamed and dusty. He remembered Wegler's little aphorism. If something can go wrong, it will. Yes indeed, Sid. It always has.

He was just leaving the room when the phone rang.

"Jason?"

"I was just thinking about you, Lois."

"I'm sorry I was such sour company last night."

"Nobody was exactly loaded with glee."

"Jason, the boy is on his way to see you. Matthew is on his way to your hotel."

"Matthew? But why?"

"I haven't the slightest idea. I don't think he talked to anyone else here. I'm quite certain of it. He asked how he could find you. He asked me not to say he had phoned me. He was very polite. Maybe he was upset. It's difficult to tell."

"I . . . I'll let you know later on what it's all about."

"All this must be very hard on him."

"Thank you for warning me, Lois. Has George phoned New York?"

"Jenny thinks he has. He's stalling. I don't know what good it will do. Her mind is made up."

Matthew arrived ten minutes later. He called on the house

141

phone. Jason said he was just on his way down to breakfast and he would be glad to have the boy join him.

The boy was waiting at the elevators. He seemed very grave and contained. They went to the dining room. He said he'd had breakfast, but he would like a sweet bun and coffee, please.

"I don't want to bother you with my problems, Mr. Brown."

"I don't know if I can help you, Matthew. But if I can, I will."

"The reason I came to you, sir, Jenny and I talked one day about the people close to her. She is very fond of every-one, of course. They are nice people. But she said some-thing about you which I remembered. She said you . . . know how to help people. She said you know what people should really do."

"I'm never that certain of anything, Matthew."

"This is something where I . . . must talk to someone who isn't really a part of it all. You do . . . know about me?"

"Yes, I do."

"I thought you might, sir."

"I learned about it seven years ago."

"Am I imposing on you?"

"No. Jenny is my friend. Don't be apologetic about this."

"It's just that it's rather difficult to talk about it, I suspect. Such a personal thing. It's easier to talk to someone I don't know awfully well, but it's still difficult. Everything seems . . . so changed for me. I see things quite differently now. I thought I was adopted, you know. My mother . . . I mean Janet . . . she was marvelously good to me, considering. And finding that my father is really my father after all. It's a bit of a shock after adjusting to it being the other way. I've been staring at myself in mirrors. I do look like him. And a bit like her. Once you know, it seems obvious."

It was, Jason realized, an extraordinary maturity for a boy of thirteen. But he had been away at school for five years, and exposed to one of the world's most comprehensive educational systems.

"I had it out with father last night," the boy said, and his voice broke slightly.

"It isn't easy for him either, Matthew."

"I realize that. He phoned Aunty Beth and explained I'm staying with him for a bit and he'll be sending me along later. He worked for a time and then came to my room. I was taping some of his discs. It's really a tremendous machine, far better than what he would have gotten me. Too good, really. I expect that bothers him somewhat. It was fearfully expensive. He asked me if he might sit down and speak with me. Father is terribly correct, you know."

"Yes. I know."

"And he is a shy man, I think. He sat down and he told me that it was a very bad age for this to have happened. Were I younger, he could give commands. And if I were older, I could be given the chance to make up my own mind about . . . things. He said that in fairness to me, he would have to talk to me as a man. And he did. It was very difficult for him. But he explained about being in New York for specialist study and treating Jenny and falling in love with her, even though he and Janet were married. But Janet was here, of course. He told her everything, and she agreed they should adopt me. But there was one part of all of it he could not explain to me."

"And you think I can?"

"I do hope you can, sir. I . . . I am fond of Jenny. She is such a warm person. Perhaps father can see just one side of it." His mouth twisted for a moment. "I do not see how a person like Jenny could have . . . given me away. Someone . . . has to help me understand that. You see, sir, Janet was very good to me. But she didn't love me. Not really. Father says that was his fault, for putting her in such an impossible situation. She would say she loved me, but she didn't. But he does, you know. Father says the . . . that life is a difficult thing and people too often end up hurting each other. Jenny has sad eyes. I thought . . . you might explain a bit of it, if you wouldn't mind too much."

The boy, behind all his poise and reserve, was pleading, Jason knew. There was rawness of new wounds there, a tremor in the careful young voice.

Jason said slowly, "I think you are clever, Matthew. I think that if I try to patronize you, you'll sense it. I think I can tell you how it was, for Jenny. It may sound ugly to you and it may be difficult to understand. I had to explain all this just the other day. To Miss Marney. She knew about it, but even after two and a half years with Jenny, she couldn't quite understand it."

"Does she now?"

"I think so. I hope so."

He told the boy about it, explaining Jenny's vulnerability and the pressures upon her, and how it must have been for her. At one point he hesitated, and then told of the other pressure on her, to have the pregnancy terminated, and how she refused. When he had finished, the boy was silent and thoughtful for several minutes.

"Thank you, Mr. Brown. Father sees it his way—as if she were too busy and ambitious to bother with a child. And I expect Jenny would see it her way—as a sort of conspiracy against her. But the truth is somewhat in between."

"It seems to be one of the characteristics of truth, Matthew. It is always somewhere in between."

The boy sighed. "Father explained why he brought her to see me. She was very determined. He wanted to prevent it. He wanted to keep me from being hurt in any way. He thought she might find me on her own, so it seemed best to bring her to the school, so that he could control the situation. But it turned out he couldn't. And I suppose that was partially my fault."

"What is the situation now?"

Matthew frowned. "Father and I have a good relationship, I think. He works very hard. I trust him and respect him. I believe we . . . are proud of each other. The point at issue is Paris. He said that as long as he had spoken to me as man to man, we should make the decision on the same basis." The boy smiled in a rueful way. "It would be easier if he were to give me direct orders, I expect. And then he . . . broke down a bit. He pleaded with me not to go with Jenny to Paris. He said he was afraid he would lose me. I asked him what was wrong with a week in Paris. He said that at first Jenny wanted to see me for an hour, but it became a day and then three days and then a week. He said she would not stop until she had taken me away from . . . everything I am used to. He sounded as if he hates her. It was distressing."

"I don't think he hates her. He may be angry at her, but I don't think it's hate. Jenny is not the sort of human being you can hate. She's reckless, but she doesn't have any real malice in her."

"He asked me to think about it very very carefully before deciding. I sat in my room, with the music, for quite a long time, until it was very late. And then I went to him and told him that if he did not want me to go, I wouldn't go. He asked if I should want him to tell Jenny. I said I would do it. I said I did want to see her again to thank her for everything, and I would tell her."

It took Jason several moments to interpret the way the boy was looking at him. He told himself his emotional reflexes were slowing down. He said, slowly and carefully, "I know Jenny very well. I think I know the sort of man your father is. And now I know you better than I did, Matthew. I think this is the very best of all possible solutions, to have you decide of your own free will to stay here. And it is the one thing Jenny would not and cannot fight."

"But it will hurt her."

"Yes, of course," Jason said. "But it is the kind of hurt she can understand. And ... if need be, I can help her understand it."

"One thinks about ... the glamor of another kind of life."

"There's one thing you may not understand."

"Sir?"

"If it became known that Jenny Bowman is your mother—and the more you are with her the more likely it is some gossip columnist will uncover it—there would be a scandal that would hurt your father's career and very probably smash Jenny's."

Suddenly the boy looked much younger. "My word! Father said nothing about that."

"Maybe he didn't want to use that kind of influence."

"But doesn't Jenny understand that risk, sir?"

"She is not a calculating woman. She is guided by her heart. I told you before, she is a reckless woman and she has found the son she lost and she loves him and that is all that concerns her."

"But I should not let her hurt herself or hurt father."

"At the same time, Matthew, she should know that your decision was not made on that basis. She wouldn't listen to that kind of reasoning."

"I know."

"That kind of scandal might make life a little uncomfortable for you too."

The boy shrugged. "That wouldn't matter."

"It might."

"A little, perhaps. I mean one doesn't wish to be conspicuous. But they would be losing things they have worked for years to obtain."

Jason took a deep breath and said, "Jenny might bring suit to regain custody of you on a technicality, a little flaw in the adoption procedures."

The boy looked horrified. "But she can't do that!"

"What if you wanted to be with her and your father refused?"

"But it isn't that way at all!"

"Jenny believes it's that way."

"There'd be no way of avoiding the scandal then, would there, sir?"

"None."

"Then she must not do it."

"There's only one person in the world who can stop her." Suddenly the boy's eyes, so like Jenny's, filled with tears. "She is a dear woman, and I do wish things might have been different. For everyone. But I shall stop her. Sir, I am very grateful to you for talking to me."

"I'm glad you gave me the chance."

"I expect she's up by now. I should phone her or go there."

"It might be better if you arranged to meet somewhere."

"Sir?"

"Some people have become curious about why she's seeing so much of you."

The boy's smile was crooked. "It was making me curious too. I understand. May I be excused now, sir?"

"Of course."

The boy started to leave, then turned back with a rather wistful expression. "In spite of all, it's going to be fearfully hard not to tell people who I am. You see, it is nothing I could be ashamed of."

"Tell her that, too."

"Yes, I guess she might like that."

Jason had no opportunity to report to Lois until early afternoon. And then he took her into the park. They sat on a low stone wall in the sunshine. It was the warmest day they'd had. The air was soft and ripe with the scents of springtime. She listened intently as he told her about the boy. She shook her head slowly, smiling, her eyes shiny with emotion. "Is it good or bad to be that mature that young, Jason?"

"Good, in this case. If he wasn't, he'd be a pawn. They'd pull him and haul him this way and that. He's dealt himself into the game."

"At thirteen I wasn't anything at all. A dumb dreamy kid. It's all misty back there. I can't remember anything with any clarity."

"I can remember I'd learned to throw a curve."

"That's really a marvelous boy. Jenny's warmth and his father's stability and wisdom. I wonder what he'll become. Something special, I bet."

"He's something pretty special right now and they both know it."

She looked at him with a strange smile. "But the people who loved me probably looked at me when I was thirteen and thought I was special."

"You are."

"Please, Jason. I wasn't fishing."

"I know. You talk about valuing yourself, but you don't."

"I'll survive."

"Shouldn't there be a little more than that, Lois?"

He felt the sun on his face as he looked at her. The gray eyes met his and slid away. Her mouth looked soft and pensive. "I did expect more. That's the standard illusion, isn't it? But you settle for what you get."

"You mean you pick up your toys and go home?"

"No. Not like that. I'm not like that. I just became a realist."

He stared at her. "I hope it's a great comfort to you."

She stood up. "Let's not start spoiling things again. Let's walk. And then I have to get back."

He walked beside her in a long silence, all too aware of her strength and beauty, her shining hair, the litheness of her stride. She was behind glass. The stopper was firmly hammered into place. She was beyond reach.

When they returned to the hotel, Ida said, "She went dusting out of here like a queen bee. A tea date with her son, yet. You could hook her smile over her ears. George is wandering around looking at the windows, picking the best one to jump through."

At six o'clock while Jason was in Lois's room helping her clip the local reviews and interviews, George came walking in with a drink in his hand. "Same old routine," he said helplessly. "Off with the kid someplace."

Jason stared at him, and he felt a little twinge of alarm. "I don't think so, George."

"You don't think what?"

"I don't think she's with Matthew."

George stared at him. "Why should there be any change? It's the same old suspense story. Will she make the theater or won't she? Why should anything be any different?"

"The boy was going to tell her he doesn't want to go to Paris."

"Doesn't want to go?"

"The boy wants things the way they were before she showed up," Jason said.

"How do you know that?"

"Matt told him," Lois said.

George looked at both of them, scowling. "And you two clowns didn't think I should know about that?"

"George," Lois said, "we were only . . ."

George Kogan smacked himself in the forehead. "So she went off and the kid hit her with that. You hit Jenny with something like that, you think she'd come crawling on back here for a good cry? You think that's the way she reacts?"

"It's something she has to work out for . . ."

"Jase, you are a meat-head."

Jason went to the phone. "Let me see what I can find out."

He called David Donne's number. A woman answered. He asked to speak to Matthew Donne. The boy came on the line and when Jason identified himself, the boy said, "What is your number there, sir. I would like to call you back from another phone."

It was five minutes before he called back. Jason asked the boy how it had gone.

"Not very well, sir. Not well at all. As a matter of fact, I botched it."

"How?"

"We met at the tea house at the Serpentine. It was most awkward at first. It was the first time I'd been with her since . . . I found out. It was difficult to talk about anything except . . . the things people generally say to one another. At last she asked me about Paris. I tried to tell her. Honestly I did. But I got as far as telling her that father was leaving it up to me . . . and she suddenly assumed that I could not possibly say anything but yes. She was so very happy, sir. She said the tickets had been bought and the hotel reservation made for me. She said she had a lot of surprises all planned. She was so very happy about it, sir."

"I understand."

"She thought it all settled. Then we went for a walk along the Serpentine, along the tow path. She said . . . we might go to see Venice too. I did not want to talk about that sort of thing. I tried to talk about ordinary things. I guess I was very upset. Finally she began to see that I was troubled. We sat on a bench to talk."

"Did you tell her then?"

"I tried to. I honestly tried to, sir, but she seemed to sense what I was going to say, and she begged me to say I would go to Paris with her. She begged me to say it. She asked me please not to leave her now. She said she needed me. Sir?"

"Yes, Matt."

"I said I would go with her. She did not leave me anything else to say. But I was terribly upset, really. I guess she could see how upset I was. I imagine . . . she realized I did not want to go with her. There's no other answer for what happened."

"What did happen?"

"Three of my friends from school appeared. Collings, Gregson and Smith Minor. They'd hired two boats from Lansbury Lido and wanted a rowing contest. They'd thought me stuck down in Canterbury. Jenny urged me to go along with them. She said she'd watch. You see, sir, she'd already told me we could have all of the afternoon together, that she was quite free. But she looked at me strangely when I set off in the boat. Most strangely. I thought she would wait. But when we were out into the lake, I looked back and she was walking slowly up the hill. When the race was ended I waited there for her for quite a long time, but she did not come back. I did it very badly. How is she, sir?"

"She's all right, Matt. Don't worry about her."

"She looked at me with such an odd expression. So . . . empty."

"I think she understands what you wanted to tell her, and why you couldn't."

"I'm going back to Canterbury this evening, sir. I would like to write her a nice letter of thanks. Do you think that would be all right?"

"I think she would treasure it, Matt."

After he hung up, he told George and Lois the substance of the conversation. George shoved his fists into his hip pockets and went and stared out the window at the dark city. "It's a big town," he said heavily. "Where do we look first? Maybe we look in that big gray river."

"She wouldn't do that to the boy," Lois said sharply.

"There are other ways to drown something," Jason said.

"What about the performance?" George asked. "Should I start canceling?"

"Do you think you should?" Lois asked.

George turned from the window. His face looked old. "I think I better wait. I better wait and hope and pray. Because you know what? It's the best chance she has. It's like the only chance she has."

twelve

JASON BROWN KNEW, before he reached his destination, that he would never forget the taxi ride to Middlesex Hospital. The message had been cryptic, and there had been no one else to take it. Lois, George and Ida had left for the theater a few moments before the call came in, and George had posted Jason in the lobby with stern orders to grab Jenny the moment she appeared, hustle her into a cab and bring her to the theater.

One of the hotel porters had led him to the proper phone. There was so much background noise he had not understood the man very well. "She has been asking for me?" he repeated blankly.

"I think you should get over here as soon as you can, sir."

The others would not be at the theater yet. And the man had hung up. He decided he could call from the hospital, and from there he could give them some more definite information.

After the pleasant day it had begun to rain again, and the night streets were all sheen and glitter and confusion of lights in the heavy traffic. He sat forward on the seat trying to will the taxi into better speed. He had a sick sense of tragic inevitability, of grisly disaster. He had told the driver it was an emergency, and the man knew the way through the complex of hospital buildings to the entrance with a sign reading MIDDLESEX HOSPITAL; CASUALTY DEPARTMENT. The word had a wartime cadence to him, a sound of aid stations and morphine ampules. It made him think of the grittily apt title on one of Irwin Shaw's short stories, "Walking Wounded." And before whatever happened to her had happened, Jenny Bowman could have been so classified. And Lois. And himself.

The taxi pulled up behind a chauffeur-driven car, and Jason thrust money at the driver and hurried up the steps, catching up to the man who had arrived in the other car just as they both reached the doorway. They went in together.

A tall young man in a white hospital coat came toward them, saying, "Oh, Mr. Donne. So glad you could come so quickly. Hope you don't mind us getting on to you, but she was asking for you, wouldn't see any other . . ."

"Are you talking about Miss Bowman?" Jason asked.

They both turned and gave him a cool and speculative look, the look that implies some social indiscretion.

"Mr. Brown?" the white-coated fellow said dubiously.

"Yes," Jason said and held his hand out to Donne. "Jason Brown," he said. "Jenny is my friend." In spite of Donne's hesitation before he took the offered hand, Jason liked the look of him. He had a look of quiet purpose, watchfulness, reliability. "Is she badly hurt?" Jason asked.

The man in the white coat looked amused. "That would not be my diagnosis," he said.

"Where do you have her?" Donne asked.

"We'd have her in an open ward if I hadn't recognized her, Mr. Donne. She insisted her name was Mudd. Miss Dreary Mudd I believe she said. I am a great admirer of hers, sir. We're trying to keep the matter entirely confidential."

"I appreciate that," Donne said.

"A female person named Landor was trying to see her a bit ago, but I didn't like the look of her and made excuses. Come along, please. We have her in a treatment room at the moment, off one of the main wards."

They followed the hospital official along a corridor with benches on either side, lined with people awaiting treatment. They had to make way for a stretcher case being wheeled rapidly down the corridor. When they reached the treatment room, the official held the curtains aside. Jenny sat on a straight chair beside a stretcher. She was looking directly at the doorway. She wore a simple dark dress, and a froth of black fur stole. Her right ankle was taped and resting on a small metal stand. Her elbow was on the stretcher, her hand supporting her tousled head. She looked mild, thoughtful, bemused and quite tight.

"My dear friends," she said. "My dear oldest best friends. I have a message and a warning for you. Never go to an exhibition of abstract art for the millions."

The hospital official had gone. Jason stayed by the door. David Donne advanced toward her. "I won't," he said.

"And if you do, don't drink the martinis."

"Definitely not." He touched her ankle with clever fingers.

"Ouch. They're half gasoline, you know."

"Did you get enough of them?"

"Enough to float Fire Island, darling. Does it show?"

"I was informed."

"By some sneak. I met a sneak too. A young Lord something. Can I take you home? Oh yes, kind sir. But it was his home he had in mind, not mine. Nobody asked me. In the general uproar I got this." She pointed at her foot.

"How did you get here?"

"A lovely lovely taxi man name of Gerald. He saw I was in need. They gave me coffee and fixed the ankle and, so help me, they want an autographed photograph for Cousin Marilyn. Which they will get. Isn't it the end. You take a drink and end up with Dr. Kildare." She made a face. "Chums, I feel wretched awful."

David saw the coffee and poured some. "Bit more coffee, Jen?"

"I couldn't get any more down if you pumped it into a vein. I'm full to the brim. Fed up to here. Fed with the whole goddamned world."

"Just see if you can wedge a bit more coffee down, dear." She looked up at him. "Have you come to take me home?"

David looked inquiringly at Jason. Jason said, "We've come to take you to the theater."

With no trace of alcohol or confusion she said flatly, "Oh no you haven't. Nobody gets me near that place ever ever again."

"I imagine they're waiting for you," Donne said.

"Tell good old George to give the money back. Tell them Jenny closed to mixed reviews."

"It's a sellout," Jason said.

"Bully for me!"

"They'll be sitting and waiting for you, Jenny. All of them."

She leaned forward to scowl at him, her eyes slightly unfocused. "Don't *wheedle* me, for God's sake! Let them wait. They want too much and I can't give it. Not any more. Everybody's always wanted too much of me. You and you and George and Ida and Lois and Herm and Sid Wegler and Aunty Beth and five thousand other people until there's nothing left to give. Nothing. I can't be spread so thin. I don't want to be rolled out like a pastry so everybody can have a nice big bite. I'm me. My own me. I belong to me, and from now on I do whatever I damn well please with myself and no questions, buddy." She got up and took a hesitant limping step, and another, and then seemed to find she could walk reasonably well. "It isn't worth it," she said in a different voice. "It isn't worth all the deaths I have to die."

"You have a show to do this evening," Donne said firmly, "and Mr. Brown and I are going to see that you make it."

She spun around to face them. "Ha! Do you think you can *make* me sing? Does George? You can get me there, but do *you* think you can make me sing, David?"

"No. I can't do that."

"I sing because I want to, not because anyone wants or makes me."

"So hang onto that," Donne said.

"I hang on good. I've hung onto every bit of rubbish in my life. And I've thrown all the good parts away. You know me, David. I'm the girl that saves the wrappings off the candy bars and starves to death. Why do I have to be the one to do that? Who elected me?"

She stood close to him. "All I know is that you're going to be very late," he said.

"I don't care," she said and sat again in the chair.

David Donne knelt beside her and put his arm around her. "Darling," he said, "I don't give a damn who you let down, but you're not going to let yourself down."

Jason suddenly realized that in their intensified awareness of each other they had forgotten his presence.

Jenny put her hand over her eyes and said, "It's so very long since I heard you call me that."

David Donne gently pulled her hand away. "Look at me. Listen to me."

They looked at each other in silence, and Jason could feel the awareness and the significance of it. He sidled toward the doorway curtains.

"Don't say anything you don't mean," Jenny said in a low voice. "If you say something and don't mean it, I'll die right here, this minute."

"I want to help you, Jenny."

"Who can help me? He didn't want to stay with me. He didn't want to come away with me. He was trying not to hurt me. But I could tell. Oh David, it was such a terrible time of revelation of . . . of how much I've lost. . . ."

"Help me now, Jenny. Help us both."

In a small wry sour voice she said, "Of course you did love me and still do and always have."

"And you've always known that."

"Then *why*? *Why!*" she said wildly.

"Right people at the wrong time. And too strong, each of us. Then making the only bargain we could . . ."

Jason slipped through the curtains. He looked into the busy ward, saw the hurry of nurses and orderlies. He waited there. The hospital sounds obscured the sounds of the voices behind the curtain. Suddenly David Donne appeared beside him. "Mr. Brown, you might tell the theater she'll be along."

"Can she make it?"

"I don't know. She can try. That's what's most important for her. She's willing to try now. I have a car here. I'll take her in. Will you come along?"

"Yes, thank you."

Jenny came through the curtains. She had fixed her hair and freshened her lipstick, but she looked white and listless. "Ready," she said in a toneless voice.

They went back toward the entrance. The man in the white coat appeared. Jason quickly gave him the theater number and the dressing room extension, and asked him to give the message to George Kogan. He went out and hurried down the steps as David Donne was helping Jenny into the car. He went around and got in beside the chauffeur.

"Palladium, Hodson," Donne said crisply. "And quickly, please."

The man was expert. He swung the car through the traffic with a hypnotic rhythm that made it all seem quite leisurely, catching the signals, gliding toward holes that opened up in the traffic pattern and closed again once they were through. Jason could hear them murmur to each other in the back seat, but he could not distinguish the words. Once he looked back for a moment and saw them sitting close, saw the moving lights on her small pallid face, on the shadowy hollows of her eyes.

Jason had thought it would be at least eight thirty before they could reach the theater, but it was just eight fifteen when he directed the driver into the lane and down to the stage door.

The stage door attendant said, with enormous relief, "Miss Bowman!"

She went along the corridor. Donne stopped Jason with a

touch on his arm. "I can't stay," he said. "But I'll be back by the time it's over. Watch over her, Brown."

"Yes. . . ."

The grave face twisted in a sudden spasm. "My God, the things we do to her! The things we ask of her!"

"You better stay until we're sure she can do it."

"I can do that. Of course. And . . . I shall be around a bit. Just until she's all right again. As all right as she can be."

Jason ran and caught up with Jenny at the mouth of the dressing room corridor. George Kogan was with her. Jason could hear the cadence clapping in the background, that universal signal of impatience and irritation.

George's face was like a stone. ". . . little ray of hope when I got the message. But look at you! There are twenty-five hundred people out there who paid money to see Jenny Bowman and you are going to disappoint all those people. Now that might not mean anything to you any more, but I still have a certain reverence for audiences, and it means a great deal to me. And if now it doesn't mean anything to you any more, then I am profoundly and genuinely sorry for you, Jenny."

She made a frail sound of despair and fled from him. George turned on Jason, accusingly. "What the hell made you think I could let her go on? She's sick and she's drunk and she's lame and she's crying. It would take an hour to straighten her out, and they won't wait that long. I've got to go out there and tell them that our Jenny is . . ."

At that moment the cadence clapping changed into a great bursting roar of welcome. George froze. His eyes went wide. "My God, has she . . ." He turned and raced through the backstage jungle to the corner of the stage, with Jason following him.

Jenny was out of reach, limping across the stage to the standing mike, wearing her street clothes, hair tousled, looking like a guilty, untidy urchin.

"Lights down!" George bawled over the uproar. "Get a spot on her. Get the walk-around mike ready." He turned to Jason and made a face. "Catastrophe. Disaster."

Jenny reached the mike. She clicked it with a fingernail. She wobbled slightly and looked owlishly at the audience as the stage and house lights went down and the spot caught her. "Hi!" she said. She slipped the fur off and held it up and stared at it. "You like this thing?" The audience did not know how to react or what to make of her. The scattered laughter sounded nervous.

"Once upon a time maybe it was a big black happy rabbit . . ." She tossed it behind her into the darkness. "Oh well. Does anybody want to forgive me for being late?"

There was answering applause, shouts of forgiveness.

"Good!" she said. "I love you." She gestured toward the wings with her thumb. "Nobody back there is ready to forgive me yet." She looked at the orchestra. "And Larry there looks dreadfully confused. He didn't get to play the overture. That always baffles him. Frankly, I've had a helluva time, and now it's time to go to work. We haven't got much organization, but we've got a lot of songs."

There was a shock wave of applause, and people began to yell individual requests. George gripped Jason's arm hard. "By God, she's got them! Somehow, she's got them."

"I'll sing 'em all!" Jenny yelled. "I'll sing every one! I'll stay all night! I don't think I ever want to go home!"

As applause continued she went and talked to Larry. The spot followed her. Someone handed her the walk-around mike out of the darkness. She gave the downbeat and the band gave her the opening to "Hello, Bluebird." Jason recognized the skill behind that selection. It was one where she could use her tipsiness to maximum effect, utilizing it and conquering it at the same time. At first her timing was off, just slightly. But then it improved and strengthened and Jason sensed George Kogan relaxing, sighing. Jason turned and saw Ida and Gabe and Lois Marney. He turned just in time to see David Donne turn and leave.

Jenny finished the song to a great warmth of applause. She nodded to Larry, and then went into her demanding number, "I Could Go on Singing . . ."

Jason turned and moved back to where Lois stood. He took her by the arm. "Come with me," he said.

"But I want to . . ."

"Come along." He took her back through the backstage area, down the steps, through the main corridor to the dressing room corridor and into the dressing room. He closed the door. But they could still hear that voice.

"Jason, you act so strange!"

He took hold of her arms. She tried to wrench free, but he held her. "Do you know what that is out there?"

"You're hurting me!"

"Do you know what that is? Can you understand what that is? It isn't any lousy little compromise based on survival."

"What's the matter with you?"

"I don't know whether you can hear me. But I have to try this. There isn't anything else to do. I'll have to go back now. And let Wegler pat me on the head like a good dog. So I don't have much time. I have to do it this way."

"Do what?"

"It isn't survival. It's a kind of marvelous endurance, Lois. What you have to do is take the risks. You have to take them all. And they turn into joy or they turn into heartbreak. But above all, you live with your risks."

"I don't know what you . . ."

"I'm a risk. I'm a lousy risk for you. I'm not a strong man. There's no shine on the armor and the white horse has a bad limp. I'm jumpy and nervous and the things I do don't turn out too well, but I have to take the risk of living. You're no tower of strength. You're sweet and scared and unsure of yourself. We're not going to find any adolescent dream of utter bliss and perfection. We'll hurt each other. People always do. But by God we'll have the rest of it too. All the plus. I want you for keeps. For permanent. With no guarantee except love."

Her eyes stopped shifting in shyness and panic and steadied on his, a gray and thoughtful gaze. "It couldn't work. Nothing works for me, Jason."

"So let's prove you right, or prove you wrong. All you do is say yes. It's a very small word. Say yes, or spend all your years wondering why you didn't. Why you couldn't."

Her eyes went wide. He held her. The level mouth softened. And then the eyes took on a heaviness. And the mouth said yes. Without a sound it formed the shape of yes, once and then again, and he took her into his arms and felt the warm strong shuddering of her body, heard the catch of her breath in something like a sob.

He heard the distant slamming surf-sound of applause and, as it dwindled, the music again, and then that throbbing clarity of the voice of Jenny Bowman singing "Alone Together." He held his scared and hearty yes-saying woman, and stroked her shining hair and kissed her temple and thought, with great smugness, with a fatuous acceptance of the corniness of it—that will be *our* song. And thought it extraordinarily sad that with all Jenny's songs and all her

singing and all the warmth and wanting of her, she gave her
songs to lovers and kept not one for herself.

THE END
of an Original Gold Medal Novel by
JOHN D. MACDONALD